Mrs. Cotts,

I told my mom once a famous quote from JD Salinger, which is "Mothers are all slightly insane." Her response was, "At one time we weren't mothers, and we were sane. You do the math." All too true.

Such a pleasure knowing the Cotts family, and I thank you & your kids for being a presence in my books. Who'd have guessed Sarah would

The Field

Stacy Riedel

BeeDubPub Independent Books
Milwaukee / Portland

have been a cover model one day??

Love, Stacy

Published exclusively by BeeDubPub Independent Books
Milwaukee, WI/Portland, OR

First Paperback Edition

Take risks, stand on principle, relinquish control, and above all
else be kind. And read books.

Library of Congress Cataloging-in-Publication Data

Riedel, Stacy

    The Field / by Stacy Riedel – 1st ed.

        p. cm.

ISBN 978-1-257-63887-1

Artwork by C. Allison, S. Potts, S. Riedel
Edited by K. Dowling

Printed in the United States of America

Acknowledgements

All the thanks in the world go to my brilliant friend, slash-and-burn editor, and brave explorer, Kati L. Dowling. Your faith in me drove this project home during many starless nights. My gratitude and pride in you is unending.

My parents certainly deserve a mention. Mom and Dad, you believed in me way back when I was pulling cons in the sixth grade, selling graph paper real estate for a quarter. You've never let me see my limits, and I owe all my grand adventures to you.

And finally, I thank every family member and friend that qualifies as a family member more than I could ever describe. I carry in my front breast pocket your secrets and unique little isms, and I love and protect them like the treasures you are. If I feel any peace, it's owed to you.

For my big sister, my Jessie.

The Field

I.

I don't take to the six a.m. hour all that great. I don't know a lot of people who do. In fact I don't trust people who do. Like those who don't drink coffee or people who make and execute New Year's resolutions with discipline, you need always worry about the thought processes of early risers. There is everything wrong with someone who sets an alarm, doesn't hit snooze, and then gets up to make a fruit smoothie, maybe goes for a jog. A blender before noon may as well be a chainsaw inside your home. They tell me it's nice to see the sunrise. I say it's nicer to imagine a sunrise, or see a picture of it in a motivational email forward.

This story starts at six a.m., obviously, because only things like what follows happen that early. I was alerted to my neighbor's crisis by both the doorbell ringing and her long, low moans. If I could imitate it I would, but then I'm not a whale seeking a mate on the ocean floor. I don't know how I knew it was her, because I'd never so much as seen her have a bad day, much less moan in any way, in delight or pain. Of course anyone who knows their neighbor enough to recognize their moan might fall in with that six a.m. group I don't trust.

I always resist the doorbell. Even when I'm expecting company, which is rare, I hold my breath a beat. In every case the bell chimes and I think to myself, "How long can I hide before they'll go away?" It's not selfishness. Maybe it is. I don't know. It's mostly the fact that anyone ringing my doorbell is one footstep away from a little too much inside my life, that is, over my threshold and nearer to my belongings. Nothing about that appeals to me.

Once my neighbor knocked just to sell me some of her kid's charity candy bars. I remember hearing the knock and quickly evaluating whether she knew I was home or not. I surmised she'd figure it out when she saw my car in the driveway, and there's only so many times I can be in the shower when she came by, only so many coincidences I can get away with. *You rang? Sorry, I didn't hear it over the football game/washing machine spin cycle/black college step team practicing in my kitchen.*

The day of the candy bars I peered though my front door's glass panels, completely forgetting that if I can see her, she can see me, and so I stared directly into her face like I was watching her on the silver screen. She stared right back and it still didn't register. She smiled, I didn't smile back. I was watching a movie after all, and you don't smile at movie stars that are looking into a camera. Finally she held up a shitty charity chocolate bar and said, "They're only a dollar!" I snapped back into reality and bought three, just because I felt guilty for hesitating. I blamed the bizarre space-out on cold medicine. I pretended to care about her kid's school trip to D.C. or homeless animals with Polio or whatever it was for, and she pretended to believe my story.

At six a.m. though I had the perfect out. I could just as easily have said I was in bed, la la land, and that's how I missed the whale moans. But if I could be guilted into buying two more chocolate bars than there are people in my home, obviously a person I know whale wailing in pain through my door is going to spur some basic human decency I swear is somewhere down in there.

I took my palms to my eyes and rubbed hard enough to actually worsen my vision, then looked into the bedside mirror. I repeated the words, "Focus, Marin. Focus." My brain caught up to reality and I heard it all at once: Honorico barking over the fence, Mrs. Lovejoy's lower lip sputtering through her weeping, the taps of her fingers against the door. I heard desperation, so I submitted. I'm not evil, I just knew whatever was on the other side of the door was surely to be far too much of her business I care to see. If the sunrise is unappealing, I sure as hell don't want this kind of hullabaloo while I'm still in my PJs.

I put on my robe and came to the door to see her, but *not* her. She was more like a zombie through the frosted glass, and I don't mean to say she looked sleepy. Her face kind of resembled those old psychedelic blob projections shot onto the wall by way of streaming light through colored gels, the sort of projectors that accompanied 70's era LSD trips, the blobs blurring together and soothing the dope user into deep breaths and heavy lids. It would have been such a welcome relief had I opened the door and realized I was on drugs instead.

No such luck. Her face was a kaleidoscope not because I was trippin', but because her face was open, flesh on the outside, blood pouring out above her lip and down her forehead in free flowing streams, all too fresh and at a volume nowhere near clotting. Snot bubbled out under her nose, she'd been crying, and it mixed in with the blood in a foamy red mustache. A new wound

for sure, but already her cheeks were swelling up around her eyes
so that she could barely see me or know I was reaching for her.
Her hair was wet and it was only when I touched her shoulder I
realized it was blood soaking her, and she wasn't wearing a shirt.
Just my neighbor, covered in terror, in a bra and jeans on my
doorstep. At six a.m. Take all that in.

I didn't know what to touch because it was all so
disgusting. Also I didn't want to hurt her, and so I was careful
reaching for her. "Nancy?" She jumped, perhaps a little shell
shocked. She tried to speak but her top lip was hanging by a
thread, and so her words were, too.

"I'm sorry," she cried hysterically. Her shoulders trembled.
Blood pooled in her collarbone pocket.

"What the hell happened, Nancy?" I could barely breathe,
but realized if she heard my nausea she would know the severity of
her meatloaf face and freak right out. She tried to mumble an
answer but made no sense. Something about a bowl and carpet,
and then a bunch of noises that got lost in her mouth before they
could be made into words.

"Come inside. You're in your bra." I let her come passed
me, helping her up the step. My hair was in its usual six a.m. light
socket mishap style, shooting in every direction as though on

watch while the rest of my body slept. I felt self conscious, then was comforted that at the moment she had more on her mind than how presentable I was.

"My feet are wet," I deciphered from what she murmured, as though that mattered at all. I sat her down in an old wingback and noticed indeed there were wet autumn leaves jutting from between her toes. I wrapped them in a blanket and took a closer look at her face. It occurred to me then this was no car accident. She hadn't been peddling her bicycle barefoot and topless and landed in the gutter. Nancy hadn't been doing some early morning rough-housing. Someone had done this to her, intentionally. And then my stomach turned over.

"Who did this, Nancy?" I examined her like a doctor, hoping to appear as though I knew how to fix her.

"Police."

"The police did this to you?!" I exclaimed.

"No," she swallowed back snotblood. "Can you please," swallow, "call the police?" Swallow.

Not a Spike Lee Joint after all, I nodded, and sprang to action just like the eyes that at the moment were bulging out of my face. I put it together. Her husband wasn't at my doorstep with her, as would any husband who had just witnessed the brutal attack of his beloved wife. So, deductively speaking, it could only be that he had beaten her. *In the face.* When a man hits a woman in the face, this is a statement as much a violent act. This is a warning of worse things to come, and a new brazen confidence. Maybe he'd hit her under her clothes and away from my judgment for years. I didn't know. I'd never seen them so much as tense. Whatever the progression, Nancy's husband was at a point now that the only next possible step was to kill his wife.

I ran and grabbed the phone, hands shaking so hard it took all the concentration in the world to execute hitting the nine, then the one, then another one. She was bleeding all over my rug, I mentally noted.

"911, what's your emergency?"

"Yes, please. I need the police." I didn't cry. I spoke solemnly, albeit making no sense whatsoever. "I need police to my home, because there has been foul play."

"Foul play, ma'am? What happened?" I heard the woman on the other end tick-tick as I spoke, typing instructions to dispatch. I'd seen plenty of cop shows to know the drill.

Chapter I.

"My neighbor is with me and she is injured, and there is a man who has hurt her." Nancy nodded. I had assumed correctly. "She will need a doctor."

"Okay, ma'am, are you safe now? Where is the man?"

"I don't know. But we are in here and he is out there and there has been some definite foul play." I was delirious.

"Alright, ma'am, I will send help to you. What is the address we can find you at?" She was very good. I felt comforted, as though she had everything under control and the foul play would be addressed. I thought to myself at that moment I would send her a thank you card. I relayed the address as clearly as I could, then asked for her badge number. "I am not a police officer, ma'am, but my name is Laronda." I wasn't even pissed she'd opted for *ma'am* over *miss* so many times during our brief relationship.

"Thank you, Laronda. I appreciate your help," as though I was talking to a bank teller. "I will ice her now." Not sure why that last part was necessary.

I hung up the phone and assured Nancy, "They're coming. Just stay here. You're safe now. No one is going to hurt you." I hoped that was true but in all honesty didn't really know. Dale could be anywhere. But she shut her eyes and nodded, hunched over so her blood dripped down her nose like rain off my roof.

"Someone has to get Michael," she warbled.

Oh shit. Michael.

"Where is he?" Her son. Eight years old. A weird kid, but only eight years old. He had a crew-cut and pronounced widow's peak and played too aggressively, but he was just a kid.

"In the house," and then she was moaning again. "We have to get him out of there!" She tried to stand, but her knees wouldn't cooperate.

"Stay here, Nance. You couldn't see him if you tried. I'll get him."

I'll get him? What the hell I was thinking, I do not know. There was a man capable of this sort of bloodshed somewhere in that house next door, possibly right outside my own at the moment, waiting to finish the job. But maybe that excited me a little. Maybe I *wanted* to confront him. Maybe I wanted to see him mess with me, someone not susceptible to domestic abuse like the beaten down dog Nancy had become, and therefore ready to kick his motherfucking ass. Maybe I wanted to clean his clock and come out of there with Michael over my shoulder like a comic book fireman. Maybe all of these things, because I never once thought about bringing a weapon with me or waiting for my back-up, the cops.

I flung off my robe and slipped into some nearby tennis shoes, opting not to tie them in the interest of efficiency. Quick and clean like a secret agent. The door flew open behind me as though I hadn't even touched the doorknob and God was personally escorting me, pushing me forward with the wind at my back. From then on the conscious me was paralyzed inside this robotic being who charged through Nancy's door and rescued her son. I wasn't me, I wasn't anyone. I wasn't afraid. My heart raced with duty, but never once did I think maybe it was a bad idea to be taking matters into my own hands. I didn't think at all. All muscles flexed and stretched involuntarily, all corners of my brain shut down to electric pulses except for that one little nugget that is colloquially known as the Ninja Control Center. We've all got it but rarely use it. We were once cavepeople after all, and the NCC is what we can attribute the survival of our species to after millions of years of primal, blind rage.

It was crisp outside, November, my favorite month most of the time since it constituted mandatory snuggles in front of a fireplace with a barrel-chested man. This year though I was single. Or I planned to be. My plan that day was to dump him. It was on the docket, right after I saved this kid's life and I got some coffee in me. But first, heroism.

I opened the Lovejoy's front door in deliberate fashion, squaring my shoulders in anticipation for my attacker. I don't know how effective I would have been. No bra, just sloppy sweat pants and t-shirt, the arms and shoulders of a prepubescent boy. But I readied myself, holding my dukes up by my chest, like a total amateur, thumbs tucked in, prepared to flail.

"Dale," I didn't ask for him. I summoned him. No answer. "Dale. I'm here for Michael. I'm not here to hurt you." I could hear my voice. It was clogged with a stress bubble in the back of my throat and so I sounded a little like Sammy Davis, Jr. minus the soft-shoe. But I was conflicted. I didn't want to swallow. He would hear that, and he would hear what a swallow implied: that I was pissing my pants where I stood. The alternative was to let the bubble sit there and keep sounding ridiculous. But that's like telling yourself not to laugh at a funeral. It's all you can think about, and the next thing you know you're grinning at a corpse. It's like ignoring a wedgie. Or a rock hard booger. I swallowed.

"I'm coming into the kitchen, Dale." Passing through the living room all appeared normal. Dim light streaming in through the curtains making their safe decorating choices that much more boring. Slate blue, tan, gray, and whatever other colors that induce yawning. Skirted, scalloped back couches straight out of a nursing home. Plaid drapes. Ruffle bordered pillows with embroidery that ranged from *I love my Golden* to an actual cross-stitch of Honorico's face, who was barking out back loud enough to be signaling the police himself.

So far no sirens though. Ahead of me was the pea green linoleum floor, scuffed by little feet, maybe Michael's, or else Nancy's as her husband dragged her around by her hair. I imagined a life in this home. It looked so ordinary from the outside. So ordinary from the inside. What a pointless display. But we all are.

I smelled sweat, and then he was there. Dale sat on a barstool in the kitchen, his feet resting on the lower rungs, his hands on his knees like he was bushed, like he was aware the police were coming for him and he didn't have a leg to stand on. His eyes were calm, sleepy even. They fluttered very slowly as I walked in the kitchen and met his gaze. "Where is Michael?" I asked him at so normal a volume, I creeped even myself out.

Dale sighed and lifted his chin toward the basement stairs. He looked down at the floor and around the room like he was taking inventory, knowing he may never set foot back in this home after that day. "Thanks," I said, which seems like a strange choice now, but at the time I was struck with a wave of gratitude, genuinely, like I was thankful he'd opted to cooperate instead of kill me. Certainly he could, Ninja Control Center or no Ninja Control Center.

The lights were on downstairs and it smelled of laundry soap. I breathed in deep, always loved that scent. I came to Michael who was standing with his hands at his sides, his eyes big and terrified. Big brown pupils and big long lashes, his little crew-cut flattened to one side from what was probably a really nice sleep. I mourned that restfulness, seeing it as the last night he would have one of those for a while. The fighting must have roused him, the cries of his mother, the grunts of his father, the names he called her, the wafts of anger billowing through the vents and down into his bedroom like a house fire. He smelled them fighting again and raced toward the scent of laundry soap instead.

Michael straightened his little racecar themed pajamas so that the shoulder was where it was supposed to be, not where it was in bed, all goofed up and twisted around while he dreamed away. He was trying to look decent. "You're okay, Michael." I reached out my hand. "Come with me."

He didn't hesitate. He tried to climb up in my arms like a koala but my NCC told me it would be impossible to fight off his belligerent father while holding a child, so I told him he'd have to walk behind me while I made sure it was safe. We stomped up the stairs swiftly, slowing near the landing to make sure Dale wasn't on the other side ready to swat me with a two-by-four.

But when we came up to daylight he was still on the stool, still on another planet inside his own mind. Then he saw Michael and came to life. "Daddy's going to jail, buddy," clearly a matter of currency in that household. He must have threatened that after every fight, when Nancy was feeling brave and ready to walk. Michael's face collapsed and he began to cry. He released his grip from my sweatpants and stood in the kitchen, waiting to choose his allegiance. What a warped existence he'd led in his short life. Choosing between the abuser and the abused, now between the abuser and the lady who bought his candy bars once.

"Michael, let's go," I barked like it wasn't optional. The kid was used to taking commands and ran to my side again. On our way out I looked to my left and caught the scene of the beating. A smashed bowl lay in shards all over the master bedroom carpet. The bed itself looked like it had been ransacked, the mattress diagonal of the box spring underneath, like they'd wrestled and she tried to run until he forced her down onto it. And then at some point he slammed a large bowl in her face, and by the looks of her detached lip, he had struck her repeatedly. That last strike must have been a doozy, as evidenced by the bowl shrapnel that would never completely be recovered in the thick tufts of carpet.

We made it outside into perceived safety, even though Dale could have just as easily shot us on the lawn with a hunting rifle as he could in the kitchen. But like in the movies, it felt like being outside meant being unhampered by anything, like there were no dark corners to be shoved into, and our cries would be heard by someone, anyone.

We first walked, then ran to my house, with steam coming off our bodies like visible tension. I looked behind us, watching our backs for murderous husbands, but he wasn't there. Just the family pick-up truck, whose license plate read DOGNUTS, which I always found humorous and wondered if it was intentionally inappropriate. Honorico was still barking, the dog they were nuts for, like he knew something was up. A memory popped in my mind of all the times I'd seen Dale walking him, a dog I found particularly unnecessary. Of course I found most dogs unnecessary, except for the seeing-eye types that assist the disabled, and of course the K-9s that are trained to tear Dale's throat out. Any other types though, the type that was there for no other utility except to be needy of walks, expensive food and medical care, I couldn't understand.

It bothered me then that in this case Dale was the more affectionate of us two, doting on Honorico during their twice daily walks, night and day, a routine of love and commitment to this submissive being. Why this submissive being and not the one that at the time was bleeding on my rug I've not yet figured out.

The police came not much long after. Sure, it was long enough for Dale to have mutilated all of our faces, even a few minutes extra to clean up the evidence and get out of town, but that didn't happen, and so when they arrived I clasped my hands together and greeted them on the sidewalk. "Thank you, thank you, thank you!"

"Who called this in, ma'am?" Again with the *ma'am*. The lady cop was 5'4" at best, but with her uniform and gear draping over the top of it she looked broader left to right than she did top to bottom.

"I did. He's in there," pointing to the Lovejoy residence.

"Who is, ma'am?"

"The assaultant." I made up a word on the spot. I've been told since that in times of stress people tend to use ten-cent words and perfect grammar, as though bringing order to chaos in any way possible. In this case I used an eleven-cent word, being that it didn't exist yet.

"Do we know if he's armed?"

"I don't know. He's in a kitchen, and there are weapons in there." The cop nodded, turned the volume low on the radio clipped to her shoulder. "Rolling pins and the like."

She asked me a couple of questions to determine the threat, know where the alleged victim was, names, timeline. When I editorialized, "he really did some damage to his wife," she shushed me with her hands. This was not court, I inferred, and I should keep my hearsay for the lawyers to say "Objection!" to. The lady cop just wanted the facts.

While they handled Dale, an ambulance arrived, and the people in it entered my home wearing their latex gloves, kneeling in front of Nancy, who at this point was verging on unglued. Her wounds still leaked like a sieve, and she shook in shock. The paramedic with the man-ponytail shined a flashlight in her eyes to assess her state, and she flinched. He spoke kindly to her, held her head back to look in her mouth for more serious damage that might restrict her breathing. The paramedics spoke to each other quietly and in terms I didn't understand, and they held her face like a Faberge egg while they counted broken bones, "one here....two...possibly a third..." Michael watched from the couch, lying on his side without any expression.

Eventually the ambulance took her away for a real doctor to examine, I gave my statement two or three times on the sidewalk out front, and Dale was arrested. Michael howled from my living room window, slapping the glass with his little hands. His father, cuffed, chin high and proud, heard the cry and answered, "It's alright, Mikey. I'll see you in a few years." He did not say this to comfort his son, but to punish all of us. He wanted Michael to know it was our fault, thereby establishing an electric fence between his son and the rest of the world. No one was safe, no one was to be trusted, no one except Dad. Not even Mom, the one whose face was at that moment being held together by God's will and sinuous threads of skin.

It was left to me to care for this kid, which was absolutely out of the question, so I took him to school under the provision a family member would scoop him up there later. We first returned to the scene to get him dressed and collect his backpack, forgetting completely to brush his teeth or comb his hair. I hadn't spent a lot of time around kids and wasn't familiar with their morning rituals, which evidently are shockingly similar to an adult's. Apparently he was supposed to have eaten breakfast and brought a lunch with him, which he only reminded me of when we were in the car. "I'm hungry," he said politely. Funny, he didn't announce any neglect to his hygiene back there.

This presented a problem. He was late for the eight a.m. bell, and I was still in my pajamas. "Oh," I looked back to him in the rearview, my big black aviators protecting me from him and him from me. "Shit," I whispered. "Are you *hungry* hungry?" He nodded. "Like, starving African child hungry?" Again, he nodded. "Okay, hang on."

I spun the wheel and took us through the McDonald's drive-thru. For breakfast I ordered him some pancakes, which he ate in my backseat in the container while I drove. When he got out I noticed there were syrupy handprints streaked across the front of his shirt, and a sticky gleam running the radius of his mouth. He seemed fine with it, and I figured this wasn't the worst part of his day, so I didn't take the pad of my thumb and clean it with my spit like I'm sure I was supposed to. He was just going to have to be a filthy kid for a day.

I tucked a lunch bag under his arm, which was really just the rest of the drive-thru spoils, one of those egg sandwiches and some hashed browns, and nudged him on his McWay. He stalled, staring at my feet. "What's up, Michael?" I asked, with a smile, like everything was fine, in a tone I couldn't mask as sincere even to an eight year old. As we know from the movies, kids can commune much easier with animals, ghost spirits, and adult bullshit.

He rocked onto his toes and hung onto his backpack straps like he was about to dive out of an airplane. His eyes were tired and overcome by the day so far. "You've got to learn stuff and then come home and tell your mom all about it." But he needed a hug, I could tell. Fuck.

Sigh.

I hugged him. It was weird. All hugs are weird, but even weirder when there's any sort of size disparity between participants. There's no way to adequately be hugged if you're the bigger of the two, and no way to hug without being consumed if you're the smaller. I reassert though that all hugs are weird, no matter what the hugger's mass is compared to mine. Their bones never line up, and I never know where to put my face. Over the shoulder? Tucked down in it? Cheek against the chest? God forbid with my mouth up against their neck, so he or she can feel me breathing. Why we want our boobs to touch and mush together to show affection, I will never understand. To me it is no less intimate than dry humping. Yet you get off an airplane and all around you everyone is doing it, publicly, with vigor. I get uncomfortable.

Weird hug over, he ran into school in that clumsy way little boys do, like puppies, stomping and clodding, no grace. I shook my head and asked myself aloud, "What the fuck just happened?"

I sat in my car and waited for my turn out of the parking lot, realizing I'd just lived a week's worth of adrenaline in the span of two hours. Nancy's face and the eyes that barely existed underneath all that black and blue, the pink and white and red and the inside-out areas of her face flesh. The Ninja Control Center signals that shot to my bones and muscles that allowed me to run into the domestic abuse equivalent of a burning building. The bowl in the carpet. The cops and their weary, end-of-shift faces. The hug. It's like I was walking out of a theater after a particularly disturbing movie, and my brain had to decide if any of it was real.

It all hit me very quickly, and all of it, even the ruffled pillows and linoleum, quieted me in a way I'd never felt before.

II.

Like I said before, I had it scheduled to dump my boyfriend. Yes, I could have saved it for a day I wasn't a little traumatized, but I am a person who checks these things off a mental list and feels cleaner and fresher as a result.

It had been coming for quite some time. Silly fights, always in public, which I'm not a fan of witnessing or being a part of.

I don't really want to know anyone's business, not if it's especially good or bad. It's obscene. I hate it when I'm out somewhere and a stranger baits me to ask about their good news. For instance when I was in the supermarket check-out line and a lady came up behind me and sighed so loud and overenthusiastically I could feel her breath tickle the whisps of hair on the back of my neck. I ignored her, it is what I do, but another stranger bit. She gushed like sweet maple syrup, *"You're* sure having a nice day, aren't you?"

To which the woman replied, "I am! My granddaughter was born this morning. I'm on my way to see her."

I didn't turn to look, but I could hear her smiling, and I found it all very gross.

Public bad news is equally repulsive. If I'm having a rotten day I keep my head down and avoid eye contact. But there's always someone who wants to talk about traffic or their flooded basement or the friend of a friend's sister's friend's friend who died tragically, and for which they want a world of sympathy. How garish. That isn't mourning. That is a loud desperation to be the most pitiful person in the room, something for which I'm not sure what the prize would be. Attention? A sense of importance? Dibs on the last piece of pizza? It nauseates me.

My boyfriend knew none of this of me and assumed I was a nice person when we first started dating. But the years had passed and despite my efforts, he could see my disinterest in this level of personal connection seeping through, and naturally that led to fights, since he cared about every damn thing too damn much.

We'd begun arguing more consistently. More regularly we were going to new places where we didn't have to talk as much, but could still say we were spending time together. The movies, the planetarium, the library, all-you-can-eat chicken wing night. A face full of food kept us blissfully oblivious.

Once we were in the art museum in a particularly austere space thick with pretension, and I wasn't so sure what the hell I was looking at. My forehead contracted. Caleb sensed my skepticism and said softly, "It's called *Hope*," squinting to read the title card on the wall.

I chuckled, a small condescending phluff escaping me. "It's just…colors." And it really was. Just colors. In no discernable pattern, or lack of pattern. I could see no intention in this thing. It looked like a bunch of paint cans had sneezed.

"You don't see it?" He was offended despite not being the artist or ever having seen the slab of nonsense before.

I tried. I really did. I took a step back and put my hands out, as though holding all of it in my consciousness at once instead of focusing on one corner at a time. I exhaled, "No. It's bullshit."

"You can't call something bullshit just because you don't understand it."

"Any piece of art I can replicate in my basement using paint and an oscillating fan is bullshit." I shrugged and moved on to the next.

But he stayed where he was, tugging me through the invisible strands of reprehension that seemed to connect us lately. "What the hell is the matter with you?" he asked, using his rolled up museum directory to point at me. "This is a person's craft, and you disrespect it just because you don't understand art?"

"You're overreacting. I don't have to like everything you like."

"You haven't liked anything since we got here."

I laughed, dug my hands in my pockets, satisfied. "I can't disagree with you there."

"It isn't the artist's fault you don't get art."

"So why did you take me here?" I demanded, raising my voice, the sarcastic smile chased off my face by the beast down below. The beast was tired of the fights that appeared to be about art, but were actually about each other's inadequacies.

I was done rolling my eyes and laughing at the sneeze painting. I was sick of it, sick of all of it. I was sick of the effort of being with him, of being in places like this with him, evaluating each other's worth based off shared interests. I was sick of being squeezed of emotion, any emotion, like the very last squirt of a toothpaste tube.

Caleb calmed himself though, sensing my impatience, trying to bring it back to art, to that painting, away from the grander scope which was essentially what he saw as my failings, and I saw as his. He came nearer and looked down the slope of his nose to me. That used to turn me on.

I remember once loving how tall he was and how that made me admire him. It's strange now to think that I ignored his obvious shortcomings because I inferred a certain personality based off his height. It wasn't a matter of feeling safe or protected, or feminine in his presence. Feeling those things required an interconnectivity I'm not sure I was capable of. No, it was just that I knew that if he was tall he'd probably gotten a lot of attention in his life, a lot of women sizing him up for breeding potential, men shaking his hand and assuming he was substantial in all ways, not just height. I figured a person sick of walking in a room and having every head turn would be a nice, low maintenance boyfriend, who didn't need to be watered or pruned. I was hoping he was a cactus, self assured, and wouldn't always have to think out loud, and wouldn't be the guy dancing with a lampshade on his head. He was good looking, tall, and through my own prejudice, confident.

Psych 101 failed me, because he was much more complex than I'd bargained for. Prickly, yes, but no cactus. Looking down onto me that day in the museum, I felt his pressure, like he wanted me to learn something. Like a parent though, not a boyfriend. It reminded me of every time I wished we could just have sex and go to bed, and he wanted to discuss it or us, or worse, get up and check his email. He had to make sure the world was still intact after that last quickie. And if it was particularly great sex, a nice long session where everyone got theirs and felt appreciated, well forget about it. There would be a play-by-play recap, and I would say in my mind, *Yeah, Caleb, I was there, too.* After which he would crank up CNN and the entire world wide web, and I would fall asleep to the low hiss of the laptop exhaust.

At the museum he lectured me, I don't know about what, I tuned it out. I concentrated instead on the embarrassment of it, because I am not an idiot or a child, and I can decide what I like. We are long passed the years of refusing to eat brussel sprouts despite never having tried them. I don't need anyone reaching into my cerebral cortex and tweaking it a hair. I knew during that lecture we weren't going to make it, and I would be dumping him very soon.

The time had come as of the day of the beating. I went to bed the night before charged and ready to drop the bomb, but unforeseen events knocked me off my high horse that morning. All day I was spinning, never quite getting my bearings, always a thought behind in conversations. I couldn't eat a bite. Not because of the blood and face guts I'd seen though. I can handle that, and I watch enough TV to know we are all the same disgusting blobs on the inside of these polished, smooth exteriors. Our topography may differ, and we may walk among each other like individuals, but let's all face it. Underneath it all, underneath our wrinkles and secret tattoos and childhood scars, we are organs, veins, and fluids of varying consistencies. We are all the same.

But we do this thing where we make ourselves special. We describe in slick ways our achievements. "Yes, I did break my nose. Thank you for asking. I got it falling down the steps while accepting my doctorate at Harvard." Or we describe our external physical oddities as though they're a burden. "If my boobs weren't so big I'd be a much better golfer," which is of course an invitation to be ogled and envied. We all do it, which makes us all even more boringly the same than I'd originally stated.

Ironically we'd be much more interesting if we just stopped talking about ourselves and being any identity at all.

Caleb and I had a plan that day to go buy the fixings for Thanksgiving. I love Thanksgiving. I love the food, falling asleep on the couch, pie, how warm my boyfriend's mother's house always was. They were a very spiritual bunch, however, and prayed before meals, especially so on holidays. I never know how to pray, so I just held their hands, tucked my chin into my chest, and waited for "amen." Once though his mother asked me if I'd like to say Grace. I'd been to dinner there enough I'd earned the opportunity. I told her I didn't know how, which made me feel a little like a piss soaked feral cat among those civilized people. But she said, "Just do your best. As long as it's from your heart, God will honor it."

From my heart. My heart is mine, and yes, I suppose if there is a God, it's His, too. But is it something to lay out next to the turkey? I went for it.

I started by greeting God. "Hello." Caleb's mom smiled. "How are you?" I looked to her apologetically, she nodded for me to continue. "This is a beautiful meal, God, sir, and it all looks like a lot of work went into it. Not just in the kitchen. You know, in the ground, too. It all had to grow and be nurtured, toiled over, if you will, to get to our table today. And in order for it to grow, there had to be an Earth, and water and sunlight. And manure. And I suppose none of that would be here without you, great God." I cleared my throat. I sensed I was rambling, which I never realize I'm doing until it's way too late.

"Aaaaanyway, God. I just want to thank you for giving us all the big things that went into making the small things, like this meal, and bringing us all together to eat. So…amen?"

"Amen," the room joined.

After dinner that year Caleb told me I'd impressed him, kissed me on the forehead, and I felt approval all around. It's rare to be the oddity in a room and feel validated for it.

But a couple years had passed and he'd forgotten how cool I could be, and it was time for me to move on. We were picking out vegetables to make a casserole we'd volunteered to bring to Thanksgiving the next day. I took a deep breath. I inhaled and just said it. "I'm breaking up with you," *POFFFF*, the breath coming out of me like it had been built up there with that sentence.

I'd learned over the years of breaking hearts that it's much easier just to say what I wanted to say. It makes no sense to build the suspense with reasons and then drop the gavel. A truly decisive person doesn't need to explain herself. It shouldn't matter why. If I've made up my mind, no explanation I give him is going to soothe or sway him. His feelings only matter so much anyway, since really in that moment I'm doing a very selfish thing, which is to preserve any days I have left in my life for things I enjoy, which by comparison could have been driving a dull ice pick into the soft spot of my temple. Having sex with an extremely obese man. Feeling the slick chunks of old milk slide down my throat. Anything was better than one more day not being good enough for Caleb, who was no prince either, believe me.

So I just said it and felt relieved the worst was out there.

Caleb put down the squash. "Here?" He was angry. Shoot.

"Is there a better place?"

"Well. Yes." His eyes got a little crazy.

"The dairy aisle?"

"Don't be sarcastic." But I wasn't being sarcastic. The dairy aisle was considerably less populated, and maybe he wanted a little more privacy.

"I'm sorry."

"But tomorrow is Thanksgiving." The supermarket was a swarm of last-minuters like us. All the buzzing around us, it seemed to me the squash pile was the perfect place, and this was a perfect time. Nobody cried in front of a squash pile, just like Grandma always says.

"If I'd waited until a day after Thanksgiving you'd be pissed off that I spent the entire holiday faking it."

"Faking it? You've been faking it?"

Exactly, "See?"

"What do I tell my mother, Marin? Are you going to tell her?"

"No," I answered without emotion. I waited for him to calm down. He was my ride home and I didn't think any good would come of me arguing with him. Arguing meant I wanted to be convinced, or that I wanted to convince him. Neither of that was any benefit to either of us. No, what we needed was a clean, surgical split. Done. No discussion. Fin.

But Caleb disagreed, apparently. His eyes welled and he looked away, hoping I'd chase him. "What do I tell her?"

I put a hand on his forearm and planted my forehead in his chest. "You tell her we broke up."

"Why?"

"That's not her business."

He pushed me away so he could see my face. "No. Why? I'm asking you why."

"Because we will never be happy." That's it. That's all that needed to be said. Clean incision.

"What?!" Nope. Rusty butter knife.

He was shocked by my statement, which still bewilders me. When consoling my brokenhearted friends, I always tell them to remember the bad times, not the good ones. Because when our egos are in tatters those bad times fall down in between the couch cushions, and like loose change and lip balm, we don't find them until months later, when we don't even need them anymore. Caleb and I had our share of bad times, undeniably. Scores of strangers had witnessed our bad times when we fought just about everywhere. But he, the dumpee, suffered temporary memory loss, or else his brain only had room enough for the bad times *or* feelings of rejection, not both.

I tried to give him a pained look that would satisfy him, a look of mourning to reassure him through his sleepless nights that I wasn't inflicting this on him, I was suffering, too, and that from different beds we were staring up at the same blue moon, aching together. Privately, in my mind, I barfed. It was all very poorly acted, but it did seem to comfort him. He held my face. "I'm happy. I thought you were."

I shook my head and looked over his shoulder, into the bright white stream of light coming in through the sliding glass doors. I felt my breathing slow as I watched it shoot through, like God, or whatever, like He was backing me up. He was telling me to hang in there, get through the conversation and then get through my life. It cast all the way onto the other side of the room, but I felt warmed by it anyway, like it was there to pink my cheeks and to go unnoticed by all the other shoppers. The beam was so intense my eyes started to see spots and trails of God, so I shut my eyes and a waft of peanuts that were in a bin next to me drifted up my nose and down into my lungs, and I was somewhere else for a second.

I came into reality and realized Caleb had been talking the whole time, and I'd heard none of it. I don't know if it was a plea, or if he was finally sticking it to me after all that time, letting me have it for all I'd led him to believe about us, that we were heading somewhere together, when it was clear underneath it all I had no intentions of taking him with me to my own personal finish line. It was my race to run, after all.

"You aren't even listening to me," I heard his voice crack.

I stared up at him, squinting. There was nothing I could say. Wrinkles formed at the corners of his eyes like he was aging where we stood. A woman reached around me for the squash Caleb had just put down. I smiled politely at her, said, "Pardon me," like a lady might. She smiled back at me, and up at him nervously. I felt rude. She didn't need to be a part of this. It was too much for a stranger to witness. She would recount this to her family the next day and say, "I think I saw a couple breaking up in the produce aisle." And then they would all speculate on what happened, this anonymous couple she would always remember around that time of year.

We couldn't finish our shopping, which had become *his* shopping after that conversation. I suggested he take me home. On the way we didn't say a word. It was only a few blocks, but it felt like miles and miles. Every red light he was a heartbeat late off the line. He drove the speed limit or slower. A woman walking her dog passed us at one point, and the dog was wearing a leg cast. Come to think of it, we never got out of second gear, and when it was clear he should shift into third, the wheezing of the engine begging for more horsepower, he would slow back down. At every stop sign he did that over-accommodating thing and allowed every car to progress through the four-way-stop before him, despite him having the obvious right of way. They would wave, and he would wave, they would wave again, and he would wave more vehemently, and then they would both inch passed the stop, then tap the breaks, then inch, then more waving. *Just fucking GO!* my insides screamed, but I was trying to get home and away without a fight. No unfinished business, no need for me to apologize, just a nice, razor sharp cut.

With the radio off, the thumping of tires in potholes as a soundtrack, the amount of time endured just trying to get the five or six blocks home, a crying baby would have been lulled to sleep. I would have, too, if I wasn't so aware of his stall tactics.

We pulled into my driveway, which was dusted with the very last of the fall leaves I'd neglected to rake. A day earlier and he would have offered to do it for me, or I would have come home to see he'd stopped by to rake while I was away, a kind gesture so as to remain relevant in my life, or to prove his love for me, which to Caleb were one and the same. I thought briefly about milking this moment, leave us hanging in limbo for a couple of days and hint toward some home repairs I'd been putting off. Not to mention those windows weren't going to winterize themselves.

I thought better of it and opened the door a smidge. "Well, I guess this is goodbye."

"Goodbye?" Again with the crazy eyes. He was apparently unclear on the notion of breaking up, that there was no need to remain on each other's Christmas card list. It was perfectly fine with me if I faded into an upsetting memory of his. It was just that final to me. It should always be final, but our tender egos tend to drag these things out far too long. Luckily mine is bigger than that, and my need for freedom usurps my need for attention. I don't need compliments, I need my side of the bed, and I certainly don't want his log of a leg draped over me. I don't need him to stroke my hair and gaze into my eyes, I need him to shut up so I can finish reading the newspaper.

He sighed. "Well, I guess I'm not missing anything." He shifted his gaze out over the dashboard, refusing to make eye contact. "It's not like I ever knew you anyway."

Huh?

He moved both of his hands to the steering wheel. There would be no last embrace, and he was officially closing himself off to me. Normally this would be a relief, but after that last statement I found myself hesitating to get out of the car.

But I did. I reminded myself how annoyed I was every time he called me "Honey Bee" in public, just to get myself to open the car door. And how whenever he gave me his psychological analysis of my parents' divorce, despite never having met them, that got me to keep walking. I remembered the bad times. On my doorstep, I watched as he drove away. I felt like smiling and waving. It's the nice, knee-jerk thing to do to people you know, whether or not you like them. But I resisted.

His words floated around my head like a cartoon dialog balloon. He never knew me? Maybe not a dialog balloon. How about a dialog bed bug, or any other blood sucker that gets under your skin. That he never knew me, that itched and burned like no other parasite.

III.

Fall settled in around me, a few weeks of chill and whooshes of dry leaves turned into dewy mornings, late night frosts, car doors frozen shut, hot coffee instead of iced coffee, a milky haze in the sky even at high noon, turtlenecks, men in turtlenecks, dogs in turtlenecks, premature Christmas lights on my neighbors' arbors. Snow was coming. Naps were uncontrollable, a drive home turning into a narcoleptic's hazard, to the point I swerved off the road a couple of times, just being insulated in my warm car and my deepest thoughts after work.

I was a little lonely. A little fat, too. Fall had settled around my waist as well.

But this is singlehood in the holiday season. I didn't regret my decision to terminate Caleb, like a lame horse, and felt a lot safer being alone than I ever had with him. I rarely thought of him, which to me was every indication what I'd done served us both. He was probably thanking me, or would soon enough. Maybe in a year or two. I felt no guilt. Just a little bit of longing for some masculinity in my life. Basically, I wanted some sex.

I will admit I don't keep a lot of friends on purpose. I keep one good girlfriend, Cherie, and one who dances on the periphery, Jane. I love Jane and think of her as someone who is better off being a bit of a mystery to me. I don't know much about her life when she isn't with me, which is nice, and mostly my impression of her is owed to the myth that I've created in my mind. I hear her life in explosive bursts, until she fades away for a time. "I'm going back to school to be an astronaut!" And then she disappears for a few months, returning to show me her degree from a European culinary institute. I'm always surprised that I can still be surprised by her.

By contrast Cherie will call and tell me in rapid fire, like it's a race, that she started her period, and how long she expects it to last, what she's craving, the severity of her cramps from one to ten, and I will respond, "Who is this?" She will ignore my joke and then go into her entire week's schedule, as though I was writing it all down, and as though her husband's beer league softball tourney was something I was thinking of attending or at the very least wanted to know every last stat about.

We are an odd group, and we all have our roles within it.

When we are all together we talk about people we know, who we're dating, goals, work. But it's nice to come together and then part with a few crumbs left of ourselves that's just our own to keep. I never understood these girls who stay up all night crying about their feelings and needing all the answers by the end of the outburst. Take a breath, I say. I doubt the sincerity of these displays, or the depth of them. It's not as though I don't cry, however if an onion can make your face leak, and so can a greeting card commercial, well, I wonder how to measure the woe-is-me's. On the scale of onion cry all the way up to death-in-the-family cry, I rank boy-trouble cries down low, right around being hit in the nose with a football.

The problem with having two good girlfriends and a bunch of fleeting acquaintances is that during the holidays they are all wrapped up in their own lives. This particular Christmas Cherie was expecting a baby, so she was decking the halls and spending an agonizing amount of time at her in-laws' place pretending to enjoy their company. "I just spent a thousand dollars on gifts. That's one thousand dollars worth of in-laws, and I only like about seventy-five's worth," she told me. And then she listed every single gift out for me, noting what she paid for them versus their regular retail price, where she got the coupon, how she wrapped them, and the great deal she got on bulk quantity double-sided tape.

Jane was traveling, because people like her did that during Christmas. She was on an airplane, I assume alone, because she is the sort of person who can get on a six hour flight and get off with three phone numbers, somewhere to stay when she's landed, and a notch in her proverbial mile-high headboard. This is all speculation, I should state for the record, since she tended to only give me raw facts, a few flights of fancy, and then change the subject. We never talk about her past, not even five minutes into her past. It's always where she wants to go, what her plans are, what she's excited about. I can't say for certainty her success rate in any of these things.

Anyway, that left me, with me as my date, my date to nowhere, to do nothing, on Christmas.

There's a bar near my house, Skud's, that I really like because it's the sort of place you can show up to in your pajamas on a Sunday morning for a Bloody Mary with an entire meal as garnish, served in what could double as a mop bucket. Or you can get all dolled up in slutty clothes on a Friday night and troll for men who aren't deserving of such effort. I go there on occasion to watch sports, or to pretend to while I overhear conversations. I like the mundane stuff, light gossip, the rhythmic back-and-forth of old friends, topical humor. Not a lot of drama, good or bad, in a place like Skud's. I sure hope it doesn't devolve into something much hipper.

I was right in assuming a week before Christmas the bar wouldn't be terribly busy. Revelers would be shopping, cooking, partying, decorating, scraping ribbon with the sharp end of a scissor and delighting over the curly q's, but complaining about it the whole time, saying Christmas has become too commercialized and who has time for all this stuff? As though they had no choice in the number of iced sugar cookies they contributed to the annual school bake sale, even though they themselves had committed to it willingly and with a bloodthirsty goal of beating all the other mothers' numbers and beating last year's total. Them, those people, they would all be out there, bitching about the incessant Christmas music, and so this bar was mine.

I walked in and noticed a pocket in front of the beer taps with my name on it. There were three free seats, and then the elbow of the bar with one gentleman sitting alone, and then a string of randoms to his right in various stages of intoxication. Off to the side a coterie of mismatched people, likely coworkers, shot darts in hideously over-conceived sweaters, reindeer earrings, elf ears, your general barf bag of holiday overdoing it. Clearly they'd all been forced to hang out for this one office party, and excessive alcohol kept them together long after it was required, in my favorite bar. They made lots of noise or else whispered about each other, to each other, and I wished I could be a fly on the wall the next morning amidst all their sober discomfort at the water cooler.

I cozied into my bar stool, getting my cheeks positioned comfortably by rocking onto the fleshy portions. With this cooler season there were plenty of fleshy portions. The bar played bluesy sex rock, the sort of music written specifically for beer commercials, the kind where women whip their hair all around, like that ever happens outside of strip clubs. The coworker ladies took the sex-rock cue and danced a little too suggestively in the company of their boss.

A bartender I recognized from many previous visits approached, smiling, "Hey, Marin. What are we having?" I had no idea his name.

"Hey, chief, how's it goin'? I'm hungry. How about a Guinness?"

"The heavy stuff, you got it." He poured my dark beer in two phases, which I always loved about it. Such a complex beer, with a specific protocol for maximum enjoyment. Skud's served it lukewarm with perfect froth, and it took three or four minutes to get the beer you just ordered. It was to be appreciated for all of those reasons, in addition to its obvious deliciousness. I liked that it required work. In dating terms it was the equivalent of going out with an emotionally unavailable man. He's high maintenance and makes you do things contrary to your value system, but God, is he delicious.

The guy on the end, the loner, wore a hooded sweatshirt and baseball cap with the ARMY logo embroidered across the front. He didn't look at me, not even to see if I was hot. This was good for two reasons. It allowed me to examine him without meeting his eye so I could make up stories in my mind about why he was there alone, what was wrong with him. Also it meant I could sit there anonymously, free of his conjecture. I realize this is unfair.

I couldn't see his eyes, but his hair under the cap was closely shorn, so I guessed he was an active duty soldier and not just a guy hoping to be mistaken for one so he could be treated like a hero and get laid a whole bunch more than normal guys. He had about a day's worth of beard growth, so I surmised he was only very recently returning home on leave, letting it all go in appropriate Santa Claus fashion. He was drinking something yellow, neat, which he took in sips, letting it burn his lips before swallowing, and then running his tongue over them. I observed his pronounced Adam's Apple, like a bobbin above his hoodie strings.

Another one of those times I didn't realize if I could see him, he could see me back. My mouth dangled open just enough until, as though in slow motion, he looked me dead in the eye. My heart thudded one giant kick of the bass drum. I gulped, and he caught that, too.

Just then, saved by the girl, one of the coworkers by the dart board appeared and flung her bony arms right around him. "Pat!" Her outfit twinkled by some sort of battery operated apparatus woven into the lining, and I couldn't tell if her sweater was a joke or not.

He was caught off guard by this chipmunk of a girl. He twisted to see who she was, an apparent old friend he'd forgotten existed since he clearly couldn't place her name. "Hey, buddy." I knew the feeling. He wrapped his big Army arm around her, leaving the other clinging to his drink like the ripcord on his parachute.

"You're home!" She bubbled up from inside herself.

He nodded, faux glee. "Yep, yep. Got in last night." Pat's smile was so brutally forced I laughed out loud, which he also caught. I tried to look away.

"Now, how long are you here? Is there time to hang out?"

"Uhhh, now? We're hanging out now." Major Brush-Off, reporting for duty. At ease, Slut.

"How about with everyone else? To catch up and stuff?"

"You know, I'm really busy. Only home for about a week."

Her blonde hair, flipped up around the bottom in a Dutch-hat sort of construction, bounced in place even when she wasn't talking. It was like watching a Chihuahua on a windy day. "That can't be true. Why not come play some darts with me?"

"Darts?" he stalled.

"You can show me how to hold it."

"A dart?"

She shrugged. "Or whatever."

Again, I laughed. This girl was good.

He pled with his eyes, looking to me for an eleventh hour save. I just grinned.

She nestled in closer to him, got serious. "Pat. You're here. I'm here. It's cold outside, warm next to me." Her eyes dropped to half moons and she beamed her drunken desires through them. Her smile flattened to a perfect horizon across her face, like the sun was setting on her dignity.

I didn't really understand his discomfort. She was, yes, like watching a hamster in a wheel, that is to say she was as complex and entertaining as a rodent. But she was also beautiful, a sure thing, and he could probably have her in his car naked within the hour. This slurry flirt was possibly the most efficient lay he could get his hands on. But the way he smiled, that family-photo teeth-only grin, the rigidity of his posture, you'd think he was staring back at a face full of herpes.

But I'm a charitable person, despite every previous paragraph that would lead one to believe otherwise, so I stepped in.

I cleared my throat. "Excuse me, ma'am?" I can inflict the *ma'am*, too. It's subtle but effective. "Pat is clearly on a date, and you're being very rude."

She broke her death grip and glared back at me, determining my worthiness of this long lost crush of hers.

"Oh." She looked back at this Pat guy, who was noticeably relieved, having reverted back to his round back, slump shouldered barstool stance. She leaned my way and said as though letting me in on some great secret, "You are one lucky girl then." Up close, in my face, her soul unfolded like ticks coming off a telegraph. I gathered every weekend, about this many Appletinis in, she was either looking for a catfight or Mr. Right, who a few more Appletinis in was defined more liberally as a male human with tinted windows, two condoms, and a roomy backseat.

"Don't I know it," I tried to convey as sincerely as possible, even though the implication of the commonly applied phrase *You are one lucky girl* is that I'm way out of my league with him. And when someone casually tells me I'm a tree sloth compared to my date, I try not to openly agree with them. But again, I was taking one for the U.S. Army here. I am nothing if not a patriot.

She whispered, "Do you know how many of us girls have totally been waiting for a shot with him? He's the one everyone wonders about."

"Oh yeah?" I chugged my beer.

"Yeah." She looked back at him. "Sooo," pausing for melodrama, "*deep.*"

"Totally, yeah," I agreed. Pat tried not to laugh.

"Totally," she purred.

"We're talking the coldest depths of hell sort of deep."

"Totally," a word she seemed to like.

"Pure hell," I deadpanned, shooting a joke right over her head like a heat seeking missile. Not only did she not get my joke, but she also failed to ask why, if we were on a hot date at Skud's of all places, there was a free seat between us, commonly known in movie theaters as the *We're Not Together Seat* more popularly employed by men with similar film interests wanting to dispel assumptions they are there on a gay date. Either she missed my sarcasm and the open seat between us because she was stupid or too drunk, or she was too occupied with giving me the up-and-down, sizing me up.

Pat pulled his hat bill lower around his eyes so the girl couldn't see him smiling at all of this. But she never took her eyes off of me, examining me. "So, Pat, this is the type of girl you're into these days?" Up and down, recording my flaws and qualities and calculating an overall margin value in her mind.

He realized he was in this now. "Yep. We're in love." I looked at him, and he was clearly loving this, in love with this scheme.

"Oh, *God*," she groaned. She pulled a lock behind her ear and bit her lip. I actually found her very pretty despite acting like a complete cow. "Well, okay," as though, assuming it was up for debate, her okay made our love real.

"Merry Christmas, dear," I condescended, not because I was invested in her or this Pat fellow, but because it's every girl's fantasy to tell off a cocky young thing in a bar. I knew the next morning she would recount the scenario to her friends in a version much more favorable to her, and spend the rest of her day eating her feelings. It was a lot of power for me to revel in and wield so enthusiastically considering I wouldn't ever see either of these people again, as I believed at the time.

"Yeah, you too," she said dryly and glided back to her coworkers in a zigzag sort of path, like a prop plane with a clipped wing. When she got back to the dart board I heard her say the word "bitch," in which context I'm not sure, though I'm certain there's no urbane way to use that word outside of the American Kennel Club. Pat and I laughed.

"I should move closer if we're going to pull this off," he suggested. His voice was low and fettered, like his vocal chords were dragging a bag of doorknobs over a gravel road. It sounded older than he looked. He scooted to the next seat and slid his drink and coaster to the big safe triangle between his elbows.

"Are you sure? You kind of looked like you wanted to be alone."

"I do, but you do, too. So it's like we're extra alone this way."

"Ah, I see. Now we're a fortress."

He nodded, "Exactly."

I smiled. I wasn't nervous. Men rarely made me nervous. I never understood the concept, why women were so shook up by good looking guys. In the seventh grade the girls would all say some idiot gave them butterflies like the boy himself was dancing around inside their bellies, and I'd say to myself that you don't feel them dancing inside your belly if you don't let them down there in the first place. In fact whenever one got close I would evaluate his assets and realize he was a high-pitched pimple factory and no one with braces should ever make me feel beneath him. All the other girls were starving themselves to be liked by the boys, while I elbowed and shot lay-ups over them in gym class basketball, a much more literal representation of who was beneath whom.

Of course then all those girls got boobs and I didn't, and it didn't matter how many threes I could hit. That confident seventh grader learned her place eventually.

"You usually come to bars and drink beers all by yourself?" he asked me with flickers of eye contact, like a shorting light bulb.

I tried to think of a cool answer. Nothing came. It threw me. I always had a cool answer. "Yeah. You?" *Fuck.*

"I just got home," pointing to his cap, "Wasn't feeling too social."

"I bet your friends here at home all ask you the same questions whenever you see them."

"Yep."

"And you have to think of different ways to answer them every time."

"Yep."

"I see. Does that mean I can't ask you any of those questions?"

He sipped his whatever it was. "I'll tell you what. You can ask one question, but that's it."

"One question."

He nodded, "So make it a good one."

There were so many. Where had he been stationed? Was he in the infantry or did he do something more technical? How long had he been in? Had he been in "the shit?" Why did he join up in the first place? Is it really like in the movies? Is his drill sergeant a total dick? How many push-ups could he do? How good did he look with his shirt off? It was hard to choose. I went a different direction.

"Why didn't you just pity fuck that girl?"

He nearly choked, coughing up that hot stinging booze enough it seemed to bubble up and water his eyes. "Not my type. She's too much."

"Too much what?" The bartender saw how far I'd progressed and started on another beer for me, winking in my direction.

Pat looked over to the girl, organizing his thoughts. At the moment she was holding plastic mistletoe over herself and was saying "is this what it takes to get some tongue around here?" She was in no uncertain terms tomorrow's regrets in embryonic form. A heavy set male coworker about 20 years too old for her snapped pictures with a masturbatory zeal, licking the corners of his mouth with the fat tip of his tongue. She pretended not to notice, then bent over and blew a kiss, letting him get just a touch too much of the shadowy part between her sweater and the bare skin underneath. She was everything every woman hates about other women, even when they *are* that kind of woman. Pat didn't need to answer my question, but I was still interested to see how he would.

"She just looks exhausting, doesn't she?" I took this in, leaning my chin on my hand and observing her more. "Exhausting to be, I mean. She seems like she burns a lot of fuel being completely purposeless." And my God, this was exactly right.

All I could do was agree with my face. I was more satisfied with his answer than the one in my head, which was closer to something like, "There is an underground plot headed by a super top secret wing of the Women's Liberation Movement whose primary objective is to wait for women like that to get in the bathtub so that women like me can throw electrical appliances in with them, preferably appliances of particularly poetic importance, like curling irons, lower-back tattoo guns, or at-home light up stripper poles." But his answer sufficed.

What a poor, hungry girl. She would always be hungry for more. Of course the primary difference between her and me was that she wasn't aware how much she was living on the outside and how little of her was left private. We are all hungry after all, we are just varying degrees of forthright about it.

"Are you meeting friends?" he asked me. He circled his middle finger around the rim of his glass and stared down into it.

"No," I breathed in. "I'm alone."

"I don't know a lot of people who go to bars alone. Girls in particular." He called me a girl. I blushed.

I wasn't bothered by what he said, even though he was extrapolating I was either an alcoholic or a lonely girl looking for Mr. Three A.M. Even if he was right about that last part there is something freeing about letting a perfect stranger know the truth about you so long as he remains a perfect stranger. It's like the satisfaction of telling a secret without any of the repercussions. I'm not Catholic, but sometimes I want to go to Confession for this exact reason. I shrugged. "I don't know what other people do. I just like my Guinness. And I like this place."

Pat didn't answer. He sipped and stared up at the muted television, which was showing a montage of the most exciting moments in sports of the week. A wide receiver caught a ball in dire circumstances and the crowd behind him erupted into hugs and high-fives as the referee gave the goal-post gesture. "I'm Marin," I smiled, extending my hand the short distance between us.

"Pat," he shook my hand and smiled, then removed his hat and placed it gently on the bar. He caught me looking at his haircut, which though too short to be smushed, had managed to be anyway.

It was a little awkward then. We'd gotten by on being anonymous, and I felt maybe I'd blown it by making us real people then. I had to be careful.

"You all set for Christmas?" he asked me.

I tilted my head and gave him some eyes. "Come on, Pat, seriously?"

"What?" he defended.

"You know how people ask you the same military questions everywhere you go? Well, I have answered 'you all set for Christmas' at least three hundred thirty six times in the last two days alone."

"You've kept quite an accurate count."

"I might be off by a couple."

"Okay, well, you got one question. I get one question."

"Yes, I'm all set for Christmas," I answered, huffing out, like it was a chore.

"That wasn't my question!" I laughed. The bartender replaced my cached beer with the new one. "I was going to ask you something else." He sipped, trying to think of another question. He clearly had nothing.

"Oh, yeah? Is it on the tip of your tongue?"

"Yes," he snapped playfully.

"Please. I'm eager to hear this."

"Fine then. You don't need to beg. My questions is," he put his fist to his mouth and pretended to cough, clearing phake phlegm. "Got a bug in there, excuse me."

I nodded. "Take your time."

"My question was," he leaned into me so he was about three inches from my nose, "what is the one and only thing you would ask for Christmas from Santa? And it can't be something that costs money."

"Wow," my eyes widened. He eased back away from me, feeling victorious. "That's an excellent question. I should have given you more credit." I thought about it. I could say world peace and make a joke out of the thing, or I could say world peace and mean it, because yes, it would be kind of nice to have that. Or I could answer with the health and safety of my loved ones, but that's boring and completely predictable. "I would want someone to decorate my tree with me." The little details of the season. We wait all year for them without even realizing it.

"You don't have anyone to help you?"

"No. My family lives out of state. My friends all have their own trees. I'm single. So it's just me and Bing Crosby, which is I guess why I haven't gotten a tree yet." It seemed so much sadder when I said it out loud.

"When do you fly out to see your family?"

I looked down and away, hoping to side-step his sympathy and change the subject. "I don't. My mom and her husband are on a cruise in the Mexican Riviera, and my dad and his wife are born again Jehovah's Witnesses."

"So no tree there either."

"No tree." I sighed and I tried hiding my feelings for my parents and their chosen spouses, keeping them down deep, somewhere around my bile duct.

"So, no family, no friends, no boyfriend. Are you alone on Christmas?"

I'd been asked this by friends and coworkers leading up to this conversation, all of them with that pathetic face you only get walking the stalls of the city pound. Every time I lied about where I was going, kind of like when I was in high school and told my mother I was staying at Lisa's, and Lisa told her mom she was staying at my house, and instead we went and had unprotected sex with our respective boyfriends in differing cabins of a docked boat.

For Christmas I told Cherie I was spending it traveling with Jane, and I told Jane I was spending it at the comfortable suburban ranch home of Cherie and her husband and their unborn baby. The lie was important until this moment at this bar, with this stranger, Pat, who deserved the truth.

"Yeah, but you know what? I'm actually really happy to be spending it alone." He nodded as though he understood completely, and I felt him sink deeper into me, staring a little harder with every word in. "It's easier to spend it doing my own thing than being in someone else's home with their traditions, and all that bullshit. It's a lot of work."

"I agree. I'm alone, too this year."

"No shit."

He grinned and I wondered what he was keeping down deep, too. "Yeah, it's great. My Dad is Army, too, stationed in

Germany. My mom died a while ago. No brothers or sisters. So it's just me. And," he held up his drink to toast loneliness, "that's the way I like it."

I clinked his glass. "Here's to a stress free Christmas."

"Amen to that."

"Thank God it isn't just me."

"It's not just you. Even though it is just you," we laughed. "It's too bad you don't have a tree though. Even if you're going to spend the holiday watching old movies in your underwear by yourself, you've got to get a tree. It's only right."

"Are you getting one?"

"Nah," he laughed.

"You really leave in a week? Or were you just saying that to get what's-her-name off your back?"

He thought hard, "Yeah. What *is* her name?" He glanced back at her, like seeing her doing that white girl freak nasty dance on a middle aged book keeper would bring back whatever high school conversation they had or yearbook inscription she wrote. It didn't work. He turned back to me. "The 26th I go back, oh-one-hundred hours." He seemed okay with that, too.

I put my hands in my lap and looked up at the screens, trying to find a tension filler. Any kind of small talk. Anything to make it less apparent we didn't know each other, but enjoyed this chit-chat cloud, and the difficulty of segueing into more conversation without breaking the code of safe solitude we'd already established we both valued. To the girl fuming at us from the dart board, this was looking like the most unromantic date between two star-crossed lovers one could possibly be on. I felt more pressure because of my awareness of her and the rolling of her eyes. Nothing came. I watched sports clips. He dug around in his pockets. I swallowed while he was distracted pulling out some cash.

He put a few dollars down and signaled the nameless bartender, who came over and shook Pat's hand in that super macho way that makes all the forearm veins bump up and out like a fault line running up his sleeve. "Good to see you, man." Fathers teach their sons to shake hands this way, and we as women watch it all our lives and marvel quietly over that little pulse of muscle that happens and then is over before our brains can really get a synapse fired. It is incredibly sexy, and it sneaks up on us.

I will admit I was turned on by this, because like Christmas tree decorations, with men it's the little things. They will crow around and try and get noticed doing the most reps in the gym or telling a story that one-ups the last guy's, but honestly it's simple stuff like handshakes that makes my peach fuzz stand up like whiskers catching a vibe. I felt a quick flash of heat shoot to my neck and armpits, and all those other secret little pockets of my body where one could smell my thoughts if they got close enough. I wondered about the forearms under Pat's hooded sweatshirt. And the biceps. And the shoulders, which had to be great if they were connected to the tree trunk of a neck I was looking at.

He caught me staring again and flashed his own fund raiser candy bars to snap me back into this dimension. "So what do you think, Marin? You want to go get a tree?"

"Now?" I answered with a slight stammer he had to have noticed.

"No. It's one a.m. How about tomorrow?"

I got the fear bubble again, like I was standing in the company of Dale Lovejoy and his gorilla rage. I didn't like it. "Yeah." I didn't smile. I was terrified. I was terrified by the fact that I was terrified. This was getting less and less anonymous. Christmas trees are intimate objects. Like toothbrushes. Photographs of my mother. Or my handwriting. I choked back the bubble, tried to go to the mindset of self-possession, shooting that basketball over that seventh grade stud and yelling, "in yo face!" It didn't work. I was sweating.

"Okay then. We'll get you a tree. We'll set it up. We'll decorate it." He seemed hesitant, but it was all his idea, which confused me. I hated that part. Men tend to do that. They bestow interest in you, but hold it reluctantly away from their face as though it reeks and drips like a spent diaper.

"Yes."

"Yes," he stuck out his hand.

"Thank you," I shook it. Like colleagues.

"For what?"

"I don't know," I swallowed again. He smiled.

"See you here at, what, six?"

I nodded. No words came out. And then he left.

The bartender waited for Pat to leave and then collected his cash off the bar. "Atta girl, Marin."

I shrugged.

Down the way the blonde was laughing hysterically. We locked eyes and she hollered in ear shot of everyone in the bar, outside the bar, my mother on her cruise ship, and deaf grannies in old folks' homes, "He shook your *hand*? What a letdown, eh, bitch? True love, my ass!" Her coworkers laughed at me, even the dowdy ones in Sally Jessie eyeglasses and big shapeless rear ends, and wiped under their eyes for migrating make-up.

I finished my beer, tipped my friend Bartender generously, and went home. I thought about my tree and Pat and nothing else, well into the wee hours.

IV.

Now let's be clear here. It's not as though I'd never had a real crush before. I have certainly had my fair share of boyfriends who I liked and liked me back, but I was never unnerved by. They were sweet but never clever enough, or smart but lacked machismo, and therefore were the sort of guy I could go places with and have plenty of sex with, but checked my external watch for our date to end and my internal watch for our time in each other's life to end. They all found me baffling but I was content. It was easier to wait for them to spoil, like milk, than to hope they never expired, like Twinkies. There are only so many Twinkies a person can or should eat. In fact anything with an unending shelf life has got to be toxic, as far as I'm concerned.

But there had only been a small number of men I truly wanted to be around, though I would never admit it aloud, and at the point in my life this story takes place, I typically avoided them like head lice. I can see pain coming a mile away. You list everything you hope for in a man, and then you meet him and instead of checking off qualifications one by one, you just circle "all of the above" and watch as your stomach sinks and the foreboding stench of a heartbreak fog creeps into your personal atmosphere.

You see, every other girl in the world circles "all of the above," too, especially the bustier ones with negative six percent body fat and questionably platinum colored hair, and the man of my dreams is sucked into the pit of subpar sirens, who drain him of all his humility and kindness, and I am left driving in my car on an overcast day with an overcast spirit, wondering if he even remembers my name, or if instead he's laughing at me and criticizing the way I look in my bra and panties, or the fact that I actually call them "underpants," and so I turn up the music and hold my breath so that none of the uncertainty waiting just behind it can come tumbling out. Because once those tears start, they don't stop for a long time. And once they do stop, girls like me harden into resolute loners who opt for holidays alone. Eventually we run into the all-of-the-above in a crowded place, flanked by hangers on, like promiscuous boogers clinging to his nose hair, and the eye contact we make tells me he appreciates me on a *different* level, but there's no reason for us to ever have sex again much less an uncomfortable conversation, as though we'd never rolled around naked together and held hands, explained that scar on his forehead or how I lost my pinkie toenail in childhood rough-housing. As though he'd never kissed that one mole no one knows about and smiled at me in a moonlit bedroom, knowing it was our secret mole.

Yes, I know this guy when I see him. Pat was this guy. But he was only home for a week, so I was safe. I did not run for my sanity.

I think I'm attractive. No, more accurately I will say that I think I'm pretty. I don't need make-up. My eyes are only brown, but men fall in love with them all the time and say my eyelashes look like feathers. My hair is naturally tousled and sexy, I don't have to do a thing to it, like I just got done flipping it back as some guy bent me over, and men look at it and think those thoughts but never say anything out loud. They just look at me in the face and wonder, and I can read them like a book, or more accurately like an issue of Hustler. My boobs are nothing to alert the censors over, but they do their job, and because of their size will always sit right up there where they're supposed to, unlike big ones that let it all go and look like descended testicles eventually. And men love my butt. Once a stranger told me it made him want to go out and buy a big bushel of peaches. Men give me these compliments, and I thank them politely and bat my feathery eyes at them, but it's

nothing I don't already know about myself. I will admit there is no
effort in this person that walks out the door, and this is half of why
I like myself better than most women.

But I am not what men want. Not really. They *say* they
want a down to Earth, self assured girl whose freckles aren't
masked under a whole other layer of face. But in fact men want a
girl they can disassemble safely, like a beginner grade pipe bomb.
They complain that women are too artificial these days, but these
are always the girls who stand between me and the guy, literally. I
see the one I want. We connect. We share a joke no one else gets,
and then exchange eye contact that melts every ice cube in the
joint. And then a girl who is wearing an outfit like armor walks up
and snuggles into his armpit, and her glare shoots me into the
shadows.

I imagine in their life together the guy first gets to see her
without that armor, whether it be her make-up or her clothes, and
he has disassembled the bomb, since essentially this is all there is
to her. When it is time to have a conversation there is very little
left to undress. Her wit runs about as deep as that first coat of lip
gloss, and so they have what he would consider a secure
relationship, which is so because no one ever reveals anything. Not
really. He doesn't have to scratch too far below her surface to
realize she is not much more than a waning case of college-years

anorexia. Who isn't? But because that is all she is, he doesn't have to contribute the failures of his life, or the crippling pain from a tragic memory, or that nothing in his life is as important as making his mother proud, though it is an insurmountable obstacle since she makes him feel like the lesser of her two sons, and he will never be good enough, etc., because all men are shouldering these things to some extent. His weaknesses remain trapped behind his eyes, and when he looks at me across the room and we don't need to speak for me to know all these things about him, he turns instead and finds the hair/tits/legs and expresses his insecurities by fucking her brains out in a public restroom.

But it is contagious, because I hide, too. I hide behind my eyes, and I find safe outlets to have sex with and attend events with. People call them my boyfriends, but I rarely say that word to describe them, just because in my understanding a boyfriend is trying out for a longer term gig, like marriage. But marriage is unsafe. So instead I say "the guy I'm seeing." It implies a transience. I see you now, but you are fading fast, buddy...

Either way I have given up on the guys like Pat, steered clear of them. This Pat though, he was quite possibly the best of both worlds.

I was nervous before our Christmas tree hunt. It happens so rarely, but when I tremble I know what that means. Inside my home, deciding between the wool cap or the ear muffs, my lower lip chattered, even though in front of the mirror it was a comfortable seventy degrees and climbing inside my unflattering puffy jacket. I saw myself shiver and grabbed my lip like I could stop it just by holding it still for a while, or massaging it, like your basic muscle spasm. But my brain seems to make an unnecessary amount of adrenaline, by a gallon at least, when I'm stimulated, maybe because I'm rarely stimulated. I can't control it or drink water to dilute it, and so my hands shake, my voice quivers, and my teeth chatter.

I went with the wool cap.

Luckily this was late December and thus an understandable time of year to be shivering, and so it would read as your run of the mill, bone petrifying, Midwestern winter chill. It would be a lie, but I was counting on lies to get me through a night with unrequited one-sided love with this Pat, this guy who represented every diss, every unrung phone, every tub of chocolate ice cream shoveled directly down below my belly button area, the part I stare at during swimsuit season and name for the last guy who put it there, like a houseguest who has overstayed his welcome. "Well, hello there, [asshole's name here]. It's time you paid rent." The

Pats of the world were directly responsible for all of this, not to mention the physical pain that I believe medical journals call Chocolate Ice Cream Gas, Chocolate Ice Cream Diarrhea, and Chocolate Ice Cream Shame, respectively.

Yes, it would take lies to have Pat and all he symbolized in my home, untangling twinkly lights.

We met at six on the button. I thought I got there ten minutes late, an attempt not to look too eager, to keep him in his place, the old upper-hand move as if to say that I was squeezing him in between other very important commitments. In fact my car radio clock ran fifteen minutes fast on account of a recent battery change, and so I actually arrived five minutes early. I could have gone into Skud's and warmed up, but my shiver would show, so I waited outside in the camouflage of my steamy breath and black cashmere scarf.

He walked up like a mountain on the move. From my stool the night before I didn't realize just how tall he was. I laughed, the only thing I could get my vocal chords to do, and he smiled a crooked smile, like only half of his mouth was working. The other half didn't want to look too eager either, I guess.

"You showed!" he announced. I smiled and hoped not to pee by accident. "I was afraid you didn't think I was serious about meeting."

"I was afraid you weren't."

"But you came anyway."

He got within a foot of me without touching anything on me, despite our parkas being about six inches worth of padding thick and presently grazing each other like visible manifestations of our very own pheromones. With that green cap he was wearing it highlighted his big square jaw and nose that looked like it had probably been broken a time or two in his manly existence. "I just really want a fucking Christmas tree." Maybe a shirtless street brawl or two? My mind wandered briefly.

He laughed, "Well, then. Let's go fill your stocking, shall we?"

I love euphemisms. I realize they're cheap. But when performed properly, on the sly, they say ten things at once. It lets us hide, I suppose.

At the lot I picked an ugly one. First, because it was the cheapest. I wasn't watching my spending for any reason except a hundred dollars seemed like a lot of money for something I would toss into the slushy, asphalt stained snow of the gutter in ten days. I couldn't justify it. At least a hundred dollar bottle of champagne is savored and consumed, and later you can make a flower vase from it. You can put it on top of your kitchen counter so that people can come and ask what in the world you were celebrating that you would have bought the good stuff, and there will be a story to tell for years, and a reliving of it just being in the presence of the bottle. But the tree gets dragged through the snow and dumped in the street for dogs to raise a leg to and then disappears into a landfill, as though it hadn't been the prettiest, best smelling thing in your home for a while there.

Pat and I bickered about this. I insisted on the ugly one, not just because it cost $17, but because no one else wanted it. I don't take to stray animals or children, but a stray tree I could do. Pat's argument was that this was the first thing I came up with when asked of my Christmas wish, and so it should be abundant and ostentatiously sized, Rockefeller Center quality, and it should smell like men's deodorant. He was so determined to get the fluffy one that he paid the guy in the red and black flannel and thick workman's gloves an extra twenty dollars to ignore me. I am smarter though, so I paid the guy first the $17, then the $83 difference for what would have made the world's most perfect Christmas tree, and then $40 to ignore Pat and strap the bony ass reject to the roof of my car before anyone would be the wiser. So in the end I paid $140 for a $17 tree that the lot would have had trouble selling at all, much less for eight times the "Or Best Offer" price. Yes, I am smarter.

Pat's eye-rolls and smug face got back to my place a short time later. I ordered pizza while he man-handled the tree and set it up in its stand, then made him do it all over again when he'd forgotten first to put down the tree skirt. He was displeased. "This thing is," pausing for the right word, "unattractive." Because it would have been uncouth to use the word "fugly."

"My grandmother made that for me when I got my first place."

"No, not the doily thing. The tree."

I sighed. "It just needs some lights and shit."

"But the doily isn't much either."

I shook my head and put my hands on my hips. "My poor, dead grandmother."

"Can't sew or pick out fabric," he replied.

I socked him in the arm, because I didn't know what else to do besides school yard flirting. He didn't even rub it.

We sat amidst the tree needles and sap glistening off the carpet and got the decorations organized. Pat checked the strings of lights for bad bulbs, complimenting me for having purchased the good strands instead of the flimsy lights from my youth that had to be tossed when even just one bulb was a leaker. I laid out my ornaments in categories: kindergarten art projects (glittery cotton balls on construction paper/crap), rites of passage (Santa in a cap and gown), travels (Mrs. Claus in a bikini, hanging ten on a surfboard), and arbitrarily themed (Elves dressed as Elvis, get it?). The pizza arrived and we discussed strategy.

"So what do you think? An equal balance of each type of ornament throughout the tree? Or should we create quadrants, keeping all the ornaments within their categorized sections?" We were spread out on the carpet like college kids, or a couple before they'd had children. I've always noticed people with children stop splaying out on the floor. They sit on couches exclusively from baby delivery on, defaulting the carpet as the kids' domain, as though plopping down there with them would be like rolling out a sleeping bag in the middle of a bison herd. Thank God I'd never gone down that path and given up my right to sit Indian style in my own living room.

"Quadrants, definitely."

"I agree." It would be like a story to tell, a history text about yours truly. All you really need to know about a person is in their tree. In fact one should never trust a person with only plain, round ornaments. That person is likely a sociopath. And if you're staring at a sociopath's Christmas tree, well, that means you're in his home and he's probably standing behind you with a fire poker. Get out of there fast.

Pat had his own judgments about my ornaments. "What is this supposed to be?"

I saw where he was going with it. "I was six when I made that."

"Yes, but…what in the hell is it?"

"It's an ornament."

"I gathered that by the hook hanging off of it, but what was your vision as a six year old?"

"It's Santa." A tennis ball, spray painted red in my dad's garage, with the words *who who who* written around its equator in chicken-scratch. "I didn't know at that age *ho ho ho* was spelled h-o."

"I think *who who who* is more fitting in this case."

"I was six."

"You keep saying that," he chuckled.

"I'd love to see what grand spectacles of innovation you created at six," I was getting a little peeved. Someone had to defend the first grade me, so tender of spirit and unaware yet how few times we truly feel we're measuring up throughout our lives.

"Actually I completed a twelve foot string of dried macaroni once."

"Amateur," I teased, bringing us back to Christmas whimsy.

Then the wine came. I'm not a huge wine drinker, but this is all people give you as gifts as an adult, particularly during the holidays. I've always written on the label who gave it to me, the date received, and what the occasion was. To me the most fun thing about wine is recalling how it got to me in the first place, and then of course the being drunk part. But wine itself isn't the romantic story connoisseurs want me to fall in love with. I don't care about the complexity. I can't tell if it's nutty or tastes like plums. I don't see it. I sip it and say, "mmmm, grapes," and two glasses in my cheeks get flushed and my teeth look Transylvanian. It's more about the memory than the wine. Unfortunately there aren't enough new memories in my real life, and so I have a cupboard full of bottles with them yet to be relived.

I read a label aloud. "Gina Poliszewski, 2008, Birthday." Pat shook his head. I read another. "Dan Levy, 2006, Housewarming." No light in his eyes for that one either. "Okay, how about this one? Gina Poliszewski again, 2005, Apology."

That one got him. "Winner."

I peeled the neck back with the knife end of my wine key, trying to recount the story. "I wish I could remember why she was sorry."

"Must not have been too serious if you forgot."

"Maybe. She's kind of a bad friend though." I cranked the screw down into the bottle, then sucked the cork up and out smoothly in a satisfying *seeerp*! "So it isn't the inconsequence of the infraction, it's more likely just awash amidst the large quantity of other infractions. I'm glad I got that out now, because that sentence would be impossible to execute a couple of glasses in."

He smiled and sipped his wine, "Here's to your shitty friend."

Things blurred from there. Things often blur when I drink, which is why we do it. Anyone claiming to drink and wake up the next day with a pristine memory isn't doing it right. What's the point?

So I don't remember the exact outline of the evening, what came when, but I know some things happened without a doubt.

For instance I know for sure outside it began to snow heavily. I know so because I came through the kitchen to get more wine and saw the frost forming in the corners of the window, steam on one side, a fuzzy two a.m. television on the other. I stared at it a minute, maybe longer, spaced out on how beautiful it was and how warm and velvety the air in my home seemed and how safe it felt, while outside it came down in 45 degree angle foofs. I breathed in a hum and realized I wasn't shivering. Might have just been the wine though.

I also remember I ate two pieces of pizza, quickly, which he made fun of. "No one's going to take it from you, you know."

"You're just jealous because I'm manlier than you," I said, beginning to slur.

"Yes, this is something you should be saying out loud," he said, being the better sarcaster of us two. He then proceeded to finish the entire rest of the pizza pie in one sitting, which I took the opportunity to note.

"What do you want to do after this? Take a three month nap in a cave?"

He answered with his mouth full, "Hey, there are starving children all over the world."

"You should have told me, I could have ordered you one of those, too." I won. He laughed. I wiped grease from his mouth with a napkin. I kissed him. I don't remember whether I liked it, but I can vividly recall the look on his face and the way his pupils blew up like supernovas, and it reminded me of when I did Ecstasy in college and stared back at myself in the mirror, trying to figure out where my eyes had gone behind those big, black, stoned spheres.

I also remember when he made fun of my hair. "You have hat head," he said plainly, the way one would tell a friend they had spinach in their teeth.

I mussed it up real good, a little embarrassed, mostly giggly. "Better?"

"Now you look like Jefferson Airplane. Wait. No. Jefferson Starship."

"That's just cold," I laughed. "Fix it." I stood in front of him just a few inches from his face. He smoothed it down as best he could, digging his fingers in it here and there to shake out the indentations, give it some life. I whispered, "That feels really good," like that orgasmy feeling you get at the salon when the girl with the fingernails is shampooing you. And then, still whispering, "I'm not going to sleep with you, so don't think of this as foreplay."

"I wouldn't be able to get passed this hair anyway." And then he kissed me, but that time I remembered every second of it, how many times his tongue was left of mine, right of mine, above it, beneath it, what it felt like to have his hands on either side of my face so that his thumbs grazed my lips as he kissed them, his fingers woven into my hair, and that when I opened my eyes for a sneak of what he looked like kissing me, he did the same, and then we laughed right on through the rest of it, and I could feel his smile as it spread out his lips into taut and happy muscles, from the generous pucker they had been. I remember every millisecond.

He behaved and I behaved, but kissing was an understood right from there on out. If he wanted to stop talking about his dad mid-sentence and lay one on me, he did. And if I wanted one last kiss before getting up to pee, I took it. We'd broken that ice, at least.

My new tree looked a little tired, its branches bending like limp celery under the weight of the decorations. But it also shimmered humbly, and we lay on our side with our wine and our hands somewhere on each other at all times, watching it reflect glimmers of glee off our teeth and back again.

I vaguely remember suggesting in a slobbery drawl that we spend his entire stay back home together and then never, ever speak again. I knew it would have sounded crazy to anyone but him, and he must have accepted, because that is exactly what we did.

V.

The next morning I woke in my bed with all my clothes on and a post-it note stuck to the outside of my pants, shielding my vagina. It read, "Too drunk. Please don't rape me." I don't remember writing it, or sticking it to my love zone, much less thinking the thought, but this was definitely my handwriting.

I woke in the first place because my alarm sounded, which again, I don't remember setting it. It squawked and buzzed like a real jerk, and in my half-sleep rationale I called it names. I said "did anyone ever tell you that you are one shrill bitch?" I mocked it, "*some*one needs to get laid," and hit snooze like I was showing it who was in charge. In the end though the alarm was queen, and I got my ass in the shower, for I had court that day.

Dale and Nancy were facing off in his preliminary hearing, where it would be determined whether she was still pressing charges, and if all was in order, he could enter a plea. I was the only other witness subpoenaed other than the responding officers, which meant I would at the minimum be giving a statement, if not eventually sitting on a stand with my hand on a Bible, just like on *Perry Mason*. I prayed court was in black and white, too.

The fuss of it was no fun, but what an adventure it seemed, and I was intrigued. I'd always wanted to see how these things worked, if a courtroom was staid and proud as in the movies, punctuated by outbursts by angry prosecutors and the hard sting of the gavel, or if it was stale and sterile like in the OJ trial, which was mostly dead air and a few salacious displays for the media, and a monotone judge under TV lights who knew not the power of clever one-liners as lofty fictional judges seem to. My curiosity brought me to court that day, pulled me there. The subpoena did, too, but more so my curiosity. I knew though the price to see it all from the inside was the possibility of seeing Nancy again. I prayed that didn't happen.

When your neighbor's face is nearly ripped off and the first time you walk into her home is to rescue her child from a potential murder-suicide, it releases into the air an odd sort of aerosol spray of forced pleasantries. Nancy had been staying with her mother ever since the event, her home still too ripe to live peacefully in, and so we had only crossed paths a couple of times. Once she came home to collect mail just as I was pulling into my driveway. I tried to get passed her with a wave, but that wasn't going to work. Her face was wrapped up like a mummy, her hair shaved at the temple to make way for those big staples that look like they could hold a whole house together. "Hello, Marin," she greeted me meekly. She was embarrassed.

I answered her in the sing-song way sympathetic people do. "Hey, Nancy, how are you?" I did not hug her. For every reason.

She tilted her head. "Yeah, you know. They gave me some pills."

"Oh, that's nice." That's nice? Her face would be scarred for eternity like the face of the moon, but at least she had Percoset.

"Yes. It's helping." Her tongue sounded fat in her mouth. "Listen, I just wanted to thank you."

I cut her off, flailing a little too vigorously, hoping to get words to stop coming out of her mouth or else wave them away like mosquitos. "No. No. That's not necessary."

She began to well up. "You saved my life." *Stop. Talking*, I demanded of her in my mind.

Again, smiling too much, gesturing at her to shut up. "It's over and everyone is okay."

But really, no one was *okay*. Alive, sure, but okay was a whole other state of being. Okay was her life with her old face, not this new, unimproved version. She just wasn't on the other side of all of it yet, as her quivering clearly showed.

It was much easier and cleaner though being the neighbor when all I had to imagine that was happening next door was how much Hamburger Helper they probably ate, the soccer practice Michael attended (because I assumed all kids his age did), which reality TV programs they watched over others they considered in poor taste. I much preferred her imaginary *okay* life to this raw version starring Meredith Baxter Birney, or some other victim-come-heroine femi-drama. I worried about the day her bandages would come off and I would have to see more than I already had. My plan was to observe her comings and goings, track a pattern, chart it if necessary, so as best to avoid her when the day came her real face was revealed.

One time I couldn't dodge her, and she popped by with muffins her mother baked for me. The card read, "You're the BEST!," and was signed by Nancy, Michael, and an actual pawprint from Honorico, who had dipped his foot in the filth of the earth before contributing his thanks. "They're pumpkin. I hope you like them." She smiled as best she could, but I couldn't help but feel like the more she talked, a little bit of her face, the bit that was showing through the gauze, was going to crack and fall off like a dying iceberg, her recovery nowhere near the point when she would appear human again. I could feel myself sweat and tried to excuse her, excuse us, but she held her hand up so I couldn't shut the door.

"Wait, someone wants to say hello." Up trotted ol' shit-toes Honorico, whose barking I had been free of since they'd been staying elsewhere. Now here he was, nose to my crotch, like he was trying to determine where I was in my cycle. Why this dog would want to say hello, or why Nancy would think I'd even felt an emptiness in his absence, was beyond me. It showed she knew as little about me and my feelings for her creature as I did about the world inside her walls all those years. I was fine with that, and so I patted his head. Patted, not petted.

Fast forward now to our potential meeting in municipal court, where we would talk with lawyers and relive the whole experience all over again, which I knew would be a nightmare. I stood in front of my closet, wondered how much effort I should put into an appearance like this. Blazer? Cable-knit sweater? High-necked blouse? The doorbell rang. "Shit," I told my wardrobe. I was presently in my bathrobe, hair a wet, mangled mess. If Nancy thought we were going to carpool, she had another thing coming.

But when I got to the door it wasn't my deformed neighbor or her son or her sexual predator of a dog, it was Pat. Pat?

"Mornin'! You look…showered." He was wearing a crisp blue buttoned down shirt, grey slacks, a shiny watch. I was confused. He inched his way toward me as though I understood why he was there and that it was assumed he could come in my home now without my inviting him. For a second I wondered how this was possible given basic laws of paranormal physics, then realized he wasn't a vampire, just a man impeding on my personal space, which in my life is equally as threatening in the light of day.

"You can't be here, I have court."

I stepped back and he shut the door behind him gently. "Yeah, dumbass, that's why I'm here." He kissed me on the cheek.

"Huh?"

He held his hands out to his side, waiting for me to know what he was talking about. I did not. "You don't remember last night when you asked me to come with you?"

"Not at all," I laughed. "All I know is my genitals wrote you a post-it note."

"Yeah, you put that there when I was setting your alarm."

I buried my face in my hands, digging my fingers into my eyes. "It's like I lost time. Like I have multiple personality disorder or something."

He looked at his watch and put his hands on his hips. "Okay, well whichever this one is needs to get dressed. We're going to be late."

"These things never start on time. I'll be fine."

He pushed me toward the bathroom. "Adults don't show up late, Marin. Hurry up."

"Jeez, yes, Dad," I blasted, then hustled into something bland and conservative enough to pass for a matzo wafer. The last place I wanted to stand out was in a building full of defendants. They weren't all there for moving violations, if you know what I mean.

On the way out to his truck I was relieved to see the driveway had been shoveled, the snow a couple feet high on either side. The night before, while we drank and later while I slept, Mother Nature had dumped a foot of the good stuff on us, leaving a crystalline fantastical world where everything, save for the road, was untouched by man and his armory of shovels and salt. My neighborhood, wrapped in gossamer and the twinkle of sunshine on snow drifts, had about a half hour of peace before the snow blowers would drone down the sidewalk and ruin everything, like a chainsaw to an old Redwood.

I scanned my driveway, pointing to it bemusedly, trying to remember how I'd carved such a geometrically perfect path in a state when I didn't have coordination enough to so much as take off my pants. "What the?"

"Someone must have done it for you," Pat answered without any need for recognition, without even looking at me. "Get in," he ordered, clicking the clicker so the passenger door was ready for me. I felt a warm rush of panic, also delight. He caught me smiling and rolled his eyes.

Court was a breeze, except for the waiting. It seemed like this was the primary purpose of a subpoenaed witness, as the hall and its wood benches were lined with people looking too impatient to be there. Everyone was anxious and inconvenienced, complaining about all the things left on their Christmas to-do list that had been procrastinated on until the last second, for which they only seemed to blame fat judges and entitled lawyers eating jelly doughnuts in the lap of luxury. One woman groaned, "I don't have time for this bullshit. I got presents to wrap. Somebody gonna answer for this." God dammit, it was her right as a tax paying American to wrap gifts, and she sure as shit wasn't going down without a fight.

The incessant sighs and complaints about "the system" were kind of ruining all the fun.

I'm not saying I loved being asked to show up at nine and then being stuck on that bench for two hours without being called, no exaggeration, just to watch suits go by. The previous night's wine sloshed around my veins like my red blood cells were enjoying a little white water rafting. I was queasy, and the vending machine egg salad sandwich being eaten right next to me by a rotund black man in a leather sport coat was far too much noise considering there was nothing crunchy on the inside. I wore my sunglasses to shield me from the offensive light shooting through the glass doors like heaven was beckoning me, which made sense considering I felt within a few points of "legally dead" on the blood alcohol ratings scale.

But I do love people watching. The glasses made it easier to get away with. I couldn't believe I hadn't thought of it sooner, worn them to Skud's at some point. "You are a saint to be here," I told my escort. "I'm sure this is worse than church," as if I knew.

"You thirsty?"

I thought about it by puckering my lips, then shook my head.

Pat yawned.

Feet shuffled. The leather bound man started in on an especially audible bag of potato chips. Pat blew out a bored, breathy "chooooooooh."

"Let's play a game," I suggested.

"Okay. What kind of game?"

"I don't know."

"Over and under on what time they finally call you in?"

"No, then we'll still just be sitting here waiting." I perused the wall of my fellow municipalians. "I got it. How about we guess violations?"

"I like it. How about this guy?" he asked grinning, pointing to a kid of eighteen at the most, who was wearing a tie and an oversized gold crucifix over the top.

"Shoplifting," I surmised. He seemed too nervous to be capable of anything more violent than tripping a rent-a-cop and running.

Pat nodded, satisfied with my evaluation.

I tilted my head toward a woman sitting directly across from me on my bench's twin. She was wearing a floral summer dress and pink socks under flip-flop sandals. The high for the day was thirty degrees. I first tried to imagine her thought process piecing it all together and deciding the outfit would read as acquittal worthy, and then I tried to figure out how she got the little flip flop loops in between her toes with those big old socks in the way. I never understood how that worked.

Pat leaned back so his gelled nub of a hairdo crunched up against the wall, mouthing to me, "Battery."

"Her?" I whispered.

"Frying pan. Husband," he mimed it for me. "Trust me."

"Hm, okay." I accepted it. Every few minutes she would pull something else out from her big canvas purse, a crossword puzzle, knitting needles, a bag of jelly beans. I figured a woman who came that prepared had been in these straits before, explaining to a judge why her husband deserved it this time.

I browsed the hall for another victim of society's ills. A man of ballerina posture and perfectly pressed slacks and boxy frame stood with his arms crossed, his legs spread to shoulder width, his neck off the charts in terms of collar circumference. "How about that meathead?"

Pat locked eyes with the guy and shared a knowing nod, neglecting to answer me.

"Is he in your platoon or whatever?"

Pat shook his head, smiled at my naïveté. "No, I can just tell. Army probably. Or Marines."

"And he can tell with you, too?"

He nodded, "Probably."

"Cool. It's like gaydar for military personnel."

Pat laughed, "Yes, because a bunch of men bunking together doesn't yield enough gay references."

It was strange. We hadn't talked much about his life outside Milwaukee. Just hadn't come up, either because I was scared to ask or because he'd artfully steered the conversation to me. "I keep forgetting you're an Army man."

"An Army man?" he balked.

"You know what I mean."

"Are you a six year old boy?"

"I'm sorry!" I blushed. "I don't know many of you."

He crossed one ankle over his knee, I patted his thigh. He winked at me. His beard was coming in quickly over two days' time, like the secret, temporary Pat peeking out of his pores. I was turned on by this. I thought of testosterone and muscles and how competitive he probably was around other men. Maybe not. Maybe he was the quiet one among his friends, maybe he was the leader. Yes, I decided, that was probably it. He was the misanthropic ruler who led by intimidation, who understood his position and responsibility, and was never, ever the sort to dance in public.

Then, like a lightning bolt an image of his penis popped into my mind, a penis bolt, and so I looked away before he could catch my giggling like a child. Like a little girl looking at anatomy illustrations in the seventh grade, laughing at what balls look like, which admittedly are still pretty funny even now, so goodness, forgive me if my eyes grow sheepish at the thought of what an unknown penis might look like up close. And then there was an image of me in a pith helmet and archaeological dig brush, staring at his undercarriage like a T-Rex fossil, and then my brain was officially out of my control.

I thought I should change the subject so as to take my internal weather vane off my lady boner. But what to think about? Baseball? That's what guys always say. Think about baseball. But then I thought about baseball players, and that was doing nothing to diminish my libido. Bats, balls, baseball butts in baseball pants, first, second, and third base. Nope. Puppies? Puppies aren't sexy. Puppies are hairy babies, so no, not at all sexy. But puppies are also a euphemism for boobs, and I definitely didn't need to be reminded of nipples, his or mine. Death? Yes, death. Genocide. War. Yes, this was working. Gross, bloody death. Thank you, Death. I was calm again.

"Question: do you feel comfortable being home? Or are you happier being away?"

Pat considered this, moving his hands to his pockets. "I don't know if it's comfort versus discomfort. This is where I come from, so it's good to be here. I'm just away from my habits. That's kind of weird."

"For instance?"

"For instance I'm usually up at odd hours when I'm in the field. Sleep is pretty irregular, just the nature of the job. On the one hand it's nice getting a full night's rest while I'm here, but it also takes some getting used to."

"I see." Probably explained why he'd spent the night next to me and my forbidden vagina, but was home, showered, and back again, before I'd even had a cup of coffee.

"I have a hard time knowing what to do with my hands." He held them out in front of him, palms up. "When I'm over there, there's usually something I'm doing. I'm usually holding a weapon. That's another thing. I feel a little jittery without my weapon." He wouldn't make eye contact. I saw his jaw tighten and flex.

"Wow. I never would have considered that. Do you feel unsafe right now?"

"I don't know if that's the word." He licked his lips, then bit one. "Maybe."

I doubted he would use that word even if it was the word.

"I have a three foot long summer sausage in my basement refrigerator if you want to carry that around while you're here."

"Thank you. That would be very helpful."

"*Meat* my day."

"Right," he humored me.

"It's a pun."

"I got it."

I smiled and he smiled, and I leaned forward so my elbows rested on my knees. He ran his hand down my back in one abrupt burst, like he didn't realize what he was doing until he was already there, and about mid-way down he was aware this was affection, and then retracted it. I took it anyway and enjoyed it for the pure impulse of it.

Just then an attorney in a suit about ten years too old came out of a small doorway and called my name. "That's me," I said to no one, like the hall of people had been wondering that whole time. I left Pat sitting on the bench.

Inside the fluorescently lit hole I sat across the way from two lawyers that knew each other and seemed to have no beef. I imagined they must run into each other a lot, just like in the movies. I wondered if they ever went out for beers, discussed any ethical reservations they faced, said things like, "Remember when we were in law school and we just wanted to save the world?" Maybe one had a drinking problem. They probably went way back.

One was the good guy, the prosecutor who obviously didn't get paid squat by the looks of his haircut. The other was the bad guy, a paid gun, not one of these state appointed schlubs. He was kind of good looking, of course, because bad guys are always good looking. He seemed relaxed, like he had this in the bag. How a wife beater could afford this guy, I do not know. Maybe Dale had been saving his money ever since the first time he hit a girl in high school, knowing that obsessive, dangerous love was a long term financial investment. Bruises ain't cheap, so maybe he'd mowed a lot of lawns to afford it.

First the defense attorney asked me to retell my side of the story, which I'd done one thousand times at this point, either to police officers, to the prosecutor in a telephone conversation the week prior, to my mother, to Pat in my inebriated gossip spree. Every time, even if part of the investigation, it felt like a lewd act revealing Nancy's grimy truth. Every time I felt like I was putting her back on my doorstep in her bra at six in the morning.

I must say though the experience is not at all like in the movies. Very disappointing. The defense lawyer didn't talk down to me or discount my tale. He nodded a lot and asked for details, nothing inappropriate. He looked me in the eye, behaved professionally and thanked me every time I finished answering his question. Mostly he wrote notes in scribbles I couldn't read even if it was right side up, and the prosecutor sat silently with his hands clasped, his mouth pursed tight. It was weird. I went to the court with imaginary spurs on, ready to fight for justice, ready to go toe-to-toe and yank a silver spoon right out of that Ivy League bastard's ass. I was full of metaphors and ready to act on them. But when he turned out to be a delightful gentleman and courteous of my time, well, I was very dissatisfied.

"So, what now?" I asked. The attorneys were content they had all the information they needed and went ahead packing their brief cases, one Italian leather, one nylon.

"Now I go visit with Mr. Lovejoy and determine his plea based off of this information and what else we have compiled," which I hoped would include the fact that we were a month from the incident and the left side of Nancy's face was still topographically comparable to San Francisco after the great quake of 1906.

"So should I stay? Or do I come back another day?"

The prosecutor touched my elbow in thanks, "You can go. If Mr. Lovejoy enters a guilty plea, we won't be needing you for future dates." Dates? Plural? "But if he enters a not-guilty plea of any sort, you will likely be subpoenaed again to testify in front of a judge."

"Okay."

"Don't worry. We'll give you ample notice so you can plan accordingly."

"Thank you. Can you tell me if Dale is out of jail? My neighbor hasn't told me much lately," possibly because I hid inside my bathtub every time I heard her drop by to pick up her mail.

"He has posted bail, but there is a restraining order keeping him from Mrs. Lovejoy and the residence. You can sleep easy." The prosecutor said this with all the confidence in the world that an invisible border that looked a lot like air was going to protect me and Nancy and her son from Dale's rage and our subsequent second-degree murders, which he would likely get away with judging by how charming his defense attorney appeared to me. He would flash his perfect chompers at that jury and they would decide I had it coming. Caleb would testify about our breakup and my inherent malice, the squash from the grocery store produce section being Exhibit A.

"I'd feel a lot better if he was wearing one of those electric shock dog collars."

"He's not coming for you, Miss," Defense Attorney O'Dimples assured me, trying to be kind.

"I can't wait until he kills me and you remember this conversation," I joked. No one found it funny but me, which isn't uncommon for my brand of sense of humor. I guess these guys dealt with actual murder all the time and had a less abstract familiarity with the topic.

"It's all going to be fine," Cheap Suit said, opening the door for me to go with a verbal shove out the door.

I shook both of their hands before leaving and smiled politely, "Go get him."

In the hall I found Pat still on the bench, looking sharp and eating a vending machine apple. He smacked away at it and smiled as I approached. "You have sexy hair," he said at plenty of decibels.

"How's your apple?"

"Tastes kind of dusty. It came shrink-wrapped."

"Can I have a bite?" He stayed seated and I leaned against him so our knees touched, crunching into the apple, looking down upon him. He wrapped his big hands around the back of my legs and squeezed me closer. "I can't believe I brought a date to court." But thank God I did.

"They going to throw the book at him?"

"Looks that way."

"That's good." I looked around me for a trash can to toss the apple core into, which Pat seemed amused by. "Jesus, you're fast. How's Nancy?"

"Didn't see her." As much as this pleased me, my stomach flip-flopped considering the possibility she wimped out on testifying. Her right as a wife was to stay at home in bed and pretend the day wasn't happening. I prayed I'd just missed her, or she wasn't due in until later. Anything but the possibility of him spooning her at that moment and telling her it would never happen again, as I hear is common with these battered women. "What do you want to do now?"

Pat massaged my thighs, hoping he would extract an idea from them. "Sleigh ride through the city?"

I thought that sounded grossly overromantic. "Nothing about that appeals to me."

"They have blankets. And we can bring some beers."

"You can see the actual poop coming out of the horses' butts." Caleb had taken me on many a sleigh ride in our time together, thinking it was going to make him the best boyfriend that ever lived, that I would brag to my coworkers about how sweet he was to do something that didn't involve him groping my boobs or watching a football game, even though he wasn't the sort of guy to be preoccupied by either of those things in any case, and so therefore wasn't at all a hero. He was selfishly forcing me to sit and watch equine assholes shoot fart steam into my direction because *he* loved the postcard of it all, not me.

"Beers and blankets in bed instead?" he offered.

My eyes shot out of my face in the shape of big bubbly cartoon hearts. "Movie day?!"

There's nothing I love more than getting a big fat blanket up over me and tucked under my chin, and sinking in and away from consciousness as whatever movie is playing on the TV nearby seeps into my dream. It is decadent. What French food is to the palate, slothing around in bed on a snowy day is to the creaky joints of a winterized body.

He stood and shook his slacks loose. Again I thought about his penis and compulsively dug my forehead into his chest. He grabbed my hair and kissed my temple. It all seemed very natural, even though on day three of knowing each other, and therefore not knowing each other, there was nothing at all natural about it. "Let's go buy some beers."

Let me be very explicit here. Though I love sex as much as the next girl, perhaps more so, and think of sexuality as a God given right and not something to withhold as though it was currency, I am not the sort to ever, ever get down to my underpants and roll around in bed with a guy on a lazy day. Even with Caleb, who had certainly seen every last fold on me, it was never in the state of our union that we could lay there and talk and laugh at old movies. Bed was for sex and sleeping, and I was fine with it having a strictly utilitarian purpose. While Caleb and I were seeing each other, I hadn't fantasized about having another person in there with me to spread out with, and migrate throughout the day so that I came to the end and found my feet dangling off the end, the fitted sheets clinging to the corners for dear life with all the huss fuss happening atop them.

So, when Pat and I got back to my place and opened a couple of beers, it was admittedly a little odd coming from me that I right away took off all of my clothes.

Let me explain how this happened.

Outside the snow sat like a crunchy top layer of crème brûlée, and from my bedroom window I looked out over the endless white field. I always love how soft it looks but isn't, and how from afar it seems so unspoiled, but up close is riddled with downed branches and pine cones, squirrel shit, tracks from whatever vermin used my field for their nocturnal workouts. I often catch myself staring out at that illusion and lose whole minutes, entranced by the big emptiness that will eventually melt down and birth an ecosystem of bugs and perennials, and I will marvel over how one can become the other. It's all so much to think about that getting lost in it, with Pat in my home and in my life temporarily, like a REM dream I become conscious of and know I'll wake from, the snow in front of me was a visible sort of white noise.

Pat came in behind me and set his beer down on the nightstand, unbuttoning his shirt absently, staring out at what I was staring at. "Pretty from here, isn't it?" He yanked his shirt tails out the back of his belt line.

"The hell are you doing?"

"Getting undressed," he answered defensively.

"You're awfully confident."

"What do you want me to do? Wear my slacks and watch to bed? Should I keep my shoes on, too?" And then his shirt was off and I could see his nipples through his undershirt. Again with the Penis Bolt. I took a swig so he wouldn't see me swallow my fear bubble again.

"Don't you have anything to change into?"

"Seriously, Marin. What would I have with me? I didn't bring flannel pajamas in the event I might get a chance to nap at the Milwaukee Municipal Courthouse." He was right. And he was unbuckling his belt. "No one says *you* have to get naked."

I held my breath and put down by beer, exhaling the words, "I'm getting naked."

I caught him swallow. "Okay."

"But you can't look." In the moment I wasn't me anymore. Not an adult with a good job, a home, a rich and storied sexual history. I was a skinny dipping teenager, cupping my tchotchke in one hand, one arm over my concave tits, diving off a dock. Terrifying and perfect.

His pants came down and he folded them neatly onto their side, draping them over my dresser. "Okay." He stood there in his boxers and white shirt, staring at me. "Go for it."

"You're looking."

"You're not naked yet."

I put my hands on my hips. "Turn around."

His eyes drooped and he stepped toward me. "Why don't I just shut my eyes?"

I wasn't falling for it, but again, the nipples. He was so close to me while I peeled everything away, the hair on his legs tickled me like flirtatious cilia. I kept my eyes trained on his as each layer fell away, but he didn't cheat, just grinned in the most torturous way knowing I was waiting for his eyes to open at my most exposed moment. He loved the power.

I stood with my top still on and lower half nearly bare. Suddenly I was aware of my mashed potato thighs. Not only had they degraded into a potato sort of color and texture, they had grown significantly into a potato shape, not as a result of intense running sprints, but because of all the pastries and saucy stews containing potatoes that had served as my interim boyfriend before meeting Pat, my seven day love, bringing with them the squishy consistency of, you guessed it, mashed potatoes. My knees clamped shut. My ass cheeks clenched.

The top was a whole other humiliation. Normally I'm the great seducer. To hell with my thighs. Off with the top, the bra will wind up wherever it does, and whichever man is on top of me will relish whatever is flopping around on my body because I am not simply giving it to him, I am taking what of his that I want. This is typically my unconscious bedroom modus operandi. I never beg him to love me, I just throw my clothes as far away from my body as possible and get to the business of getting sweaty. He is typically refreshed by this approach, and so I have a 100% success rate getting a man to have sex with me. It is truly remarkable, I know.

But this time I was a fumbling moron. Paranoid of him being so close to all my skin, my plan was not to take the pullover sweater off first, and then unbutton the top underneath notch by notch. That would have made a lot of sense. However in the interest of efficiency I thought it better to consolidate the layers into one and pull them both off at once, right over my head in a sleek swoosh. Good idea, except I hadn't calculated ahead of time how narrow the two tops combined become, and how big my cranium and sexy head of hair was, and how cumbersome it was all going to look if he opened his eyes and I was standing there in my underpants, my thighs and my bra, and my arms and head concealed, trapped helplessly in the prison of my own drab sweater combo. Yes, very efficient.

I let out a little grunt, struggling to get the collar passed my chin. If I could do that I would be naked. He sensed a hindrance. "You want some help?"

"Absolutely not," I answered from inside my sweater. "Are your eyes closed?!"

Pat laughed, "Why do you sound muffled?"

I waited for him to stop snickering. "I'm stuck." His hands came to my body then, sliding up my sides like a blind person seeking out a doorknob. He traveled up and discovered my arms in a high "V" over my head, feeling the contours of my face through my sweater. I growled in frustration.

"You have no idea how hard it is not to make fun of you in this state." Pat maneuvered the sweater this way and that, first pulling my left sleeve by its cuff like a sausage casing, then the other. Together we carefully freed my chin and off the rest of the sweater popped, like a dump flying without warning out of a horse's rear end.

I came out of there and into the light of the room and realized the worst. He was staring right at me. "You look wild," he said. My hair was less Diana Ross and more Sideshow Bob after that fiasco.

"You saw everything." He had. I could see it in his eyes. He looked far too amused to have abided by the rules until then. "You were pretending to keep your eyes shut?" He stepped up against me so that my bra met his undershirt. I kept my hands at my sides, shielding the broadest part of my thighs. "What a violation."

"That was the worst strip tease I've ever seen in my life."

Pat was kind not to be staring directly at my little boobies, but I know men. Their vision rivals a fly's. It may seem like eye contact, but part of their periphery and 96% of their brain power are trained on whatever skin is showing, calculating how heavy you're going to be on top of him.

"Can we get into bed now?" I was tense. I was not the smoking hot superstar of sex that bedroom was used to seeing.

"Same time?"

I tucked my mouth into itself so he couldn't see my lips, and nodded. He put his hands on the outside of my shoulders and rubbed them briskly, using his body to say *calm down, dork, you're overreacting*. Why was this so easy for him? Why was it so hard for me? Is this why women have casual sex with bargain basement bar-close losers? Because they're lucky to have us, no matter how mashed our potatoes are? All I know was this wasn't me. I was supposed to be running the show. I was supposed to be swan-diving off the dock while all the other kids watched, tchotchke and concave tits proud and bare, not slipping in behind some shoreline brush.

Then at once he jerked us both sideways into bed so that we landed with a bounce, and then scurried under the blankets to safety. He let out a blissful moan and dug his feet into the mattress.

"I love cold sheets." Pat smiled at the tops of his toes that were tent-poling the duvet.

I was quiet.

He didn't touch me right away, but I heard his head turn on the pillow and look at me, which to me at that short distance and nearly naked, was the same as touching me. I did not reciprocate.

"Hey, eyelashes, what's the problem?" I shook my head. I hated that I shook my head. My heart was beating hard in a way that concerned me. Then, like my handsome push pin, he busted right through the protective balloon I'd blown up around me. He rolled onto his side and put his palm over my heart, pausing to assess. "I could practically hear it over there." I still said nothing, just tried to normalize my breathing. I realized then my chest was rising and falling with the intensity of a mating grizzly bear. Not the look anyone should ever be going for. "Are you okay?"

If having my sweater stuck wasn't humiliation enough, I was now cusping on an anxiety attack, and my eyes teared up. In a room I'd had plenty of naked sex in, with more attractive men than Pat, where I'd dominated my partners and stood boldly at the helm of the ship like I was spearing a whale, why was I now freaking out? He wanted to know if I was okay, but I did not answer him. I couldn't.

"Hey. Look at me." I wouldn't. "You need to look at me. I can help you." The breathing was worse now. My teeth were chattering. There was no cold air to mask it then, in fact my armpits felt like two buttered corn cobs. And then it all came at once and I was there in full blown panic. I hadn't had one of these since I heard through my childhood bedroom wall that my parents were divorcing, and that my dad was a "fucking cheating bastard," knowing full well what that meant even in my gentle innocence. I remembered that feeling my whole life, praying it wouldn't come back. I could handle the divorce and my father's betrayal, but I couldn't handle losing symbiosis of my central nervous, circulatory, and respiratory systems. If I lost control of those, I lost control of everything. There is nothing scarier than feeling like a passenger in your own body, and I was determined my whole life never to be in a position again when that would wash over me against my will.

But it did that day. Somehow I rolled onto my side to face him, one boob crushing the other. Pat was composed, my eyes were big like a lemur's, and my forehead was sore. He took my two fingers and put them on his jugular sweet spot, digging them in real good so I couldn't miss the rhythm. He put his right arm around me and held my lower back firmly, tugging me close to him, like he was what was holding me from a tumble over the edge. "You're going to hyperventilate if you don't focus on my breathing."

He was calm, on task. I felt his heart beat against my fingers in thick, solid thuds. "Match me," he said low. His mouth was three inches from mine. I could feel his breath when he spoke, like a blown dandelion tickling my face.

I shut my eyes and tried to slow to his beat. It worked. I felt his chest move like a tide and imagined myself on the water, on an anchored boat, rocking up and down in time with the waves, the beat coming through my fingers and shooting up my arm into my own heart, my taptap slowing a little more to a tap tap, and then a tap... tap, and then the taps easy and spaced out enough they seemed singular. I opened my eyes. The tears subsided, but I was still sweating.

So I kissed him. This was not the sort of kiss that treads delicately, like the opening acknowledgements in this book. I skipped right passed that and jumped to the arc of the story, where I dive right in with my tongue and lips hot and swollen, which from a side angle is slow, and hungry, like our mouths are seeking out more of each other, like we want more than there is available. It was less a kiss and more an attempt to consume each other. He moved his hand to my hair and brushed it away and off my cheek. I felt him move to my neck, his fingers dipping into the pit of my collarbone, and then his hand pushed my shoulder so that I was on my back. The full weight of him sunk onto me, and I loved it, pulling him tighter with my legs.

After this day I tried so hard to remember the details. Flashes of him taking inventory of my body popped into my memory. The pain of his hip bones against mine. The eye contact we made for one split second. When he smiled at me. When he held one of my hands over my head and clutched it like he was afraid of fumbling. But I don't remember it all. I really, really wish I could. Living in the moment though, you are on a different level of consciousness, and you are more than any other time of your life inside your own body. You aren't thinking about how you're perceived, or what you should be doing. You are sitting with God inside a dream, thanking him for having come up with this sex stuff way back when.

It's all mostly a haze, but I can hear him clear as a bell in my memory saying, "How long are we waiting?" through a tongue kiss, somehow maneuvering his boxers off before the question even ended. I answered through raspy breaths, "Not a second longer." And then I shut my eyes and fell in love with him.

VI.

Day three we woke up together.

Any time I've had someone in my bed with me, however long the guy stayed after our sex, I turned my back to him. Part modesty, part manifestation of my fierce independence, part your-purpose-is-served-now-get-the-fuck-out-of-here-already, I typically wanted not to see his face after having seen everything else of him just a few minutes prior. Sometimes they overstayed their welcome, so I pretended to be asleep until they had shit to do and left on their own accord. This was the least messy and required the least amount of conversation, however once I told an old boyfriend, "Thank you. Here are your pants." *Thanks for the sex, now get out of my face.* Sometimes I don't have time or energy to lay there and fake snore.

With Pat though, we woke up nose to nose. Our breath was rancid, a little like the scent of a rotting skunk that got stuck underneath my sun room one summer and died, which happened to be on record as the most humid summer in seventy six years. In short, we were unappetizing. I woke up first, flicking my lids a couple of times just to get a quick read of him, and then shut them again to evaluate the situation. I suddenly became aware of where I was and plotted to turn away.

But he roused before I could, breathing in a whoosh like he had been holding it all night and was now gasping for life. We went to bed exhausted. The entire day and night before we had lots of sex. I lost count. We watched *It's a Wonderful Life*, which I was able to recite every line of, but didn't because I know that's annoying to others. He got up and made grilled cheese sandwiches at one point and served them to us in bed on one plate. He ate three, I ate one, feeding the beasts. We talked. He asked me things, like why I live so far from my parents, why I didn't have a boyfriend, who I call when my car breaks down, what that one book was that made me fall in love with all other books, what I think God is, if there is one. I asked him things, like how his mom died, what he would do if he had to spend a million dollars in one day, why the Army, what the perfect three a.m. bar close food is, and if he ever stops to think whether he's lonely in his life. He was, as much as me, mostly alone.

In and out of naps, movies, those light fingers down each other's backs that feel like cat whiskers and make your arm hair stand on end. It had been a long, bleary day.

That morning, after having revealed easy things and hard things, after him kissing the notch above my butt crack, and having seen my face go ugly just as I'm reaching nirvana, I was suddenly self conscious. We were both far too naked, and far too much information floated around in low hanging clouds, fogging up the windows and frizzing my hair.

We laid there on our bellies and stared at each other. No words at first, just taking stock of what we both looked like first thing in the morning. He had some crust in the corners of his eyes, but otherwise could put on clothes and leave the house looking handsome and ready for anything. He looked at my lips (chapped), then my nose (pillow creased), then my eyes (puffy). He slid his hand palm-down underneath my belly, tucking it in there for safe keeping. My eyes squinted into a smile. In the silence it felt a little like those last few ticks up a roller coaster before it tips down into potential death.

"You know what's crazy?" he asked me. I loved his voice first thing in the morning. It sounded like every passage was blocked, like it was painful to speak. Like I was waking up next to an old coal miner. I realized there were a select few who'd ever heard that voice and wondered just how many.

"What?" I eeked out through the driest vocal chords in existence outside of the Sahara.

"You were once a sperm."

I laughed in my typical morning baritone.

"Like, one little sperm. Just a tiny sperm."

"Don't forget I was an egg, too."

He rolled his eyes. "Such a feminist." He moved his hand to my hair and wove a finger around a wave like he was twirling spaghetti. "Now look at you."

"I've come a long way."

"You don't think that's crazy? How we go from that to this?" He was talking, and I know it was real, but I felt like I was dreaming. "First you're DNA. And then you become this five-foot-six person."

"Five-foot-seven," I corrected.

"Five-seven." He examined me down to the freckle. "You don't think about that ever? Once you didn't even have thoughts. You were like this little nothing. No thoughts."

"Yep. And now all I do is think."

"Yeah. First you're a sperm…"

"And an egg."

"Yes, and an egg." He smiled. "And you're swimming, but you don't even know why you're swimming. You don't care. You don't have the *ability* to care. Get your head around that."

I finished his thought. "And then years later you're watching a football game, and you're analyzing plays, cheering or booing. And while that's going on, I don't know, maybe you're thinking about what you want to eat next, or how long you can hold it before you have to go pee or something. First you can't think at all, and then you're five-seven and you're thinking and feeling a ton of stuff all at once." I considered for a second which I preferred.

He stared at me, no expression. "From a sperm in a sack, to the guy with the sack."

I hid my face and laughed, "Gross. But yes. And then you get old and die."

I wanted him to kiss me. He didn't. He spoke, which was fine, too, since I mostly only loved what he ever had to say. "If you're lucky." But he lied. Nothing about Pat wanted to get old and die.

Later he went home and dressed. I showered and washed the him off of me, and the me off of me, a mish-mash of skin cells, hair, body fluids, and everything else that is disgusting in any other scenario. I was sore. Standing in front of the mirror afterward, I counted the bruises. Two like fingerprints low on my waist. One on my left shoulder. Two big ones that darkened by the minute on the dips between my hips and pubis bones. Those ones hurt the worst, so much that I suddenly stopped taking the ability to walk for granted.

In an instant I loved them all, found them all very sexy, and knew they'd be gone in a week, and I would be sad. I would miss them. I considered taking a picture of them, then realized how ridiculous I was being. I noticed what was happening and vowed not to sink too far into this guy. He was temporary for a reason.

Our plan on day three was to go to church. I realize the irony in this being that we were the least pious people to walk through the doors that day. But Pat was raised Catholic, I was raised an earth child whose religion was love, although that was never specified, so I just counted on being really polite to get me to heaven, or wherever. Things went pretty undefined all those years growing up, so I'd had a real curiosity for that whole church song and dance since I was young.

On television you see everyone in their finest go to these big, beautiful cathedrals in a very pedestrian sort of way, like the building itself doesn't steal their breath, nor does the gravity of what it represents, and that the structure is ground zero for all that exists and all that matters in their personal constitution. Sometimes on Sunday mornings I run out and grab doughnuts, and I drive slowly by a church near my home just to watch all the people coming out, the kids skipping like they've been pardoned, a look of relief to be detached from something so heavy. I envy it, and then I go home and eat my doughnuts alone.

I told Pat these things in between sex two and sex three, so he offered to take me to St. Josaphat's Basilica. Traditionally Polish, it had become a place Catholics went to see and be seen by God during the holidays, Milwaukee's most venerated of religious hubs. Round the clock Mass had begun, mostly only the older crowd attending at first, the younger folk suffering through, picking their noses and spacing out. On a Friday afternoon, after some pancakes and coffee at a shitty downtown diner, we could blend in with these revelers, so long as I kept my head down.

He gave me the rundown. Before we left the house he told me what I needed to know to at least get in the door without an old man with a scepter standing on a pedestal and pointing it down to me, bellowing, "Tourist!" with such fury the stained glass shivered in fear. The sign of the cross, the kneel, how to look reverent and humble but still maintain a cool like I'd been doing that choreography my whole life. He suggested I skip Communion, if it was being offered while we were there. Staying seated and seeming repentant would actually make me appear more devout, not to mention I would surely out myself being face to face with Father Whatshisname and not know the rhythm and flow of Communion, which to me should be an awkward exchange considering a veritable stranger is putting food directly into your mouth. It never is though. A well-oiled machine, everyone knows their part.

"Just don't smile," Pat ordered.

"You can't smile in church?"

"It's not like it's outlawed, but no, we're not going to a party."

"But it's Christmas. We're celebrating."

"No, we're not."

I was seriously confused. Still am. "It's Jesus' birthday."

"Okay, well, when you walk in and don't see streamers and balloons, don't be surprised."

"Fine. No smiling. Got it. But no frowning either, right?"

"You're thinking way too hard about this. Just stay close to me and do what I do."

Good plan.

I'd seen the Basilica a million times from the freeway, wondered what kind of upkeep it took to maintain such a monolith. The window washers, the clergy, the landscapers, the money. It was an icon of the Milwaukee skyline with a very distinct dome among the more prevalent steeples that shot through the old oaks and birches like desperate pleas to be noticed. St. Josaphat's though is the kid in school who shows up one day with a mohawk. It is a force.

Up close I hid in the church's shadow. Plopped in the city among the run-down homes and shops, it stood as a fortress. I couldn't imagine even the most angry of neglected youths wanting to graffiti the side of this place. I felt its power just driving along side of it, which I suppose was the intention all those years back during the construction of it. The mission was to give the Catholics somewhere to go, give them something to remind them of their irrelevance in the grand scheme of history, yet their responsibility as part of it, and to show the Protestants who's boss. Give it the enormity of an old courthouse, subtly echo the pitch of their roofs, columns, and the asceticism so that worshippers know whatever the letter of the law says, the real buck stops there, with ol' Saint Joe.

I was terrified.

Luckily Pat dressed me. I would have shown up in a veil if I hadn't known any better. He expressed to me the importance of being just this side of respectful without being showy. We settled on a knee-length grey wool shift dress and black crew neck cardigan with pearly buttons, stud earrings, pantyhose, and a thick heeled pump. In the car I patted down my hair and applied bobby pins wherever it was acting out, fearing its innate sexiness would get me booted. "Are you worried about Jesus being mad at you for taking me there?"

"I think Jesus wants people to come to church."

"Yeah, but I'm an outsider." A doubter. A nay-sayer. I said God and Damn in the same sentence two, maybe three hundred times a day, even just for paper cuts.

"You know nothing about Christianity." He looked over his shoulder to size up a particularly tight spot to parallel park into.

"I know, I know. Jesus is nice. But I'm not going there to be converted." *If last night was any indication.* "I'm going as a spectator. I'm exploiting Jesus."

"How much cash do you have in your purse?" he asked while cranking the wheel right.

"I don't know. Twenty bucks."

"Put your twenty in the collection plate and call it even." Simple as that. He stuck his tongue out to get us situated just right in between two minivans, then looked me in my troubled face. "You're thinking too hard."

"Okay."

"Now how do I look over there?" he gestured to the curb side of us.

I checked the side mirror. "Perfect fit. Like a finger in a butt."

He shook his head. "You can go ahead and get that out of your system now."

Chapter VI.

We crossed into the church just fine. The threshold didn't sting or sizzle as I stepped over it, my pantyhose didn't melt into my skin. I kept Pat's big arm in front of me, gripping his hand so that half of my body was concealed while we walked. It was a slow afternoon, just the die-hard Jesus lovers showing up with their beautiful inherited rosaries, a few old crows in lunch lady shoes and matching scowls. We found a pew midway up, which was quite a haul from the entry. Pat knelt, then me, giving my gesticular shout-out to the Father, Son, and the Holy Spirit. We slid in away from the aisle and sat in silence a moment.

My goal going in was to observe, but once we were there I had so many questions. I wanted to know everything, all of its history. Who built it, when, why, how it was funded, how many men died during its construction, if it's haunted by anyone other than Jesus. I wanted to find a guy in a robe and sit him down with a notepad and pen and fire away my queries. But I couldn't, and so I sat there in awe.

The dome from the interior is drama on the level of an Italian opera. I imagined a person a century before with a monocle and a pencil stuck in his beard, mapping out the design, saying to himself, "Too busy?" The amount of detail, the commitment to perfection, on the scale that a single set of eyes couldn't take it all in at once, I was meek underneath it. I wished I'd had a pamphlet or something to fill my head with answers while it busied overflowing with wonder.

I couldn't hold it in. I whispered, "I feel like I'm in the Grand Canyon."

He nodded, keeping his gaze forward, his chin tucked slightly.

I could have blubbered. "I'm choked up."

Again he nodded.

I studied the joint. Up front nothing important was happening. A woman, an employee of God, shuffled around organizing papers and books on a big wide podium adorned with enough gold leaf filigree, Liberace would have called it too gaudy. "Who's that lady on stage?"

"It's not a stage," he whispered back to me. He pulled down the kneeler and settled in to pray.

Seemed awfully stage-y to me.

I knelt with him and crossed my hands in front of me, trying to look less conspicuous as I spied on the others. Nearby a man of about two hundred years old prayed softly in another language, something Baltic. He sat in his modest suit, his knees too worn to abuse anymore, his head held low in deference to the inevitable end that was coming for him. I wondered if he prayed more or less as his years passed. Then I wandered to his background, which country he came from and what he remembered of the mother land, his regrets, what he'd seen, and why he took comfort here, of all places in a church, where all his secrets couldn't be denied.

I thought about actually praying, too. It's not like I had nothing to ask or be thankful for. I just never know how. There's no show when you're talking privately with God, and I've never known how to bring down the curtain.

"Do you go to church over there?"

He leaned his head closer to me. "Over where? Overseas?"

"Afghanistan."

"Not really. They hold services, but I only go when I really need to."

I imagined what constituted "needing to." What did it take? Probably some horrible, brain staining shit he wouldn't ever say out loud. "Do you pray over there?"

"Of course."

"What do you pray for?"

He shrugged. "The basic stuff. Safety. Gratitude."

"Forgiveness?"

"Sure."

I thought to myself he must feel some conflict. In our short time I'd learned he'd fired his weapon plenty of times on several fronts in two different countries. He told me the day before while we were ass up and genitals down in bed that most of the time he wasn't sure if he's hit anything, particularly at night. My heart stopped when he told me a war story, thinking of the brittle security of night battle, how quickly control turns to chaos and the fear associated. He must have become numb to this fear, or would have to in order to be effective at his job. I found it all very sad.

"He knows you're doing your best, Pat." I said this even though I wasn't sure there was a He, or that anything he did in any country was being recognized by any higher governing body. After all, the enemy thought God sanctioned their killing, too. It was more likely in my mind that Pat was floating along on a big ball called Earth in this universe, and history here mattered as little as history on some other planet we would never reach or ever know about. Whatever kept him up at night is less likely something he would have to reconcile with God over and more likely a forgotten nothing blip in time no one that no thing would ever care about or remember, this planet or otherwise. How important we all seem to be in our own minds.

But Pat appreciated the sentiment anyway and looked at me in thanks.

"No smiling in church," I told him.

He waited to gather his thoughts, then said, "I mostly pray to understand."

"Understand what?"

"A lot of guys pray for their families, but I don't have kids or a wife. Or that all the men come back okay, but I know what we signed up for. So I pray for the stuff no one else is praying for. I figure we need that the most, to understand the big picture, whether or not what I'm doing is getting us to a positive result."

He was too smart a guy not to ask himself that question and hope God was listening.

I thought I could challenge him on this or answer the damn question myself, my being pro-peace in a different way than Pat was, a way I believed was the correct way. But then we were in church, where everyone was pro-peace, however each person defined that. Some guys went over to fight, because all their life they'd preferred to fight over sitting still, whether that be at home as a kid or abroad as an adult. But I knew Pat was different. He went over there with some purpose in his back pocket, and whether that had been altered by what he'd seen, I had no idea. He didn't appear to waver in his commitment, that was certain. If he doubted anything, it wasn't of where he was supposed to be, and there would be no convincing him otherwise. And besides, you don't have a political debate at St. Josaphat's. You don't steal all the attention at Jesus' birthday party.

We prayed, or appeared to, for a few minutes. Somehow we went unnoticed.

"Can I make an observation?" I asked.

"Yes."

"You don't appear homesick."

"Okay."

"You don't miss this at all?"

"Church? No. I don't miss church."

"I mean home," he knew I meant home. "This is everything you know. And yet you act like it's a chore to be here."

He dropped his hands and looked at me. "I left for a reason, Marin. Maybe I don't want to be around everyone I know."

"You mean every*thing*."

"That's what I said."

"No, you said everyone. You don't want to be around everyone you know." I dipped my head so he could see the presumptions I was making.

He shook his head and said, "Yes, Dr. Psych Von Analysis. Don't read into that too much."

But nobody misspeaks. "Fine. So you don't miss anything?"

He thought it through a while, trying to come up with an interesting answer, any answer at all. "I guess Halloween."

"You don't dress up or anything over there?"

"No. I forgot it had even passed until someone showed me a picture of his kid in a costume. Dracula or something."

"I love Halloween."

He nodded. "Me, too. What was your best costume?"

"When I was a kid I thought it would be funny to be a piece of candy *asking* for candy."

He chuckled, "How old were you?"

"Eight or nine."

Which he found even funnier. "That's a good sense of irony at such a young age."

"I was a Hershey Bar. My mom painted a big appliance box in brown and silver and made holes for my face and arms. It turned out great but I could barely walk. I had to kind of shuffle around since there was no room for my knees to bend. I got to one house and had to trick or treat from six feet from the door since I couldn't get up the step."

"That is hilarious."

"My dad told me to fart inside it to see if it made a funny sound, which it did. Except then it had nowhere to go, so I basically hot-boxed my fart right in there with me." Pat made a low, fake fart with the corner of his mouth, supporting me. I laughed in a whisper. "Luckily my farts are so pleasant they're like a gift to the human race."

"Prove it, fart right here."

"I'm not farting at St. Josaphat, Pat."

"Farting *with* St. Josaphat," he clarified.

Finally we excused ourselves on account of being barely capable of containing our laughter, fake farts, or general fart humor. We did our best to prolong our ruse until we reached the door and freedom. In the arctic air we smiled and our teeth froze. He wrapped his big bear paw around the back of my neck and said, "Check that one off the list."

We ran to my car, my scarf blowing behind me like a flag, dodging ice patches along the way. Once inside we sat with rock solid faces, our cheeks having hardened in the cold. I grabbed his hand and leaned halfway over the center console. He met me in the middle and kissed me. "I propose Halloween."

"You propose Halloween?" Pat flattened my hands into blades and then rubbed the outside of them, blowing down in between them.

"Yeah, you didn't get Halloween. You miss Halloween. Let's do Halloween."

He leaned back and started the car. "Okay."

"Tomorrow," I lowered my voice to the gritty affect of a grim reaper, "we welcome the dead."

VII.

You'd be surprised what a deal you can get on Halloween decorations during Christmas time. At the drug store orange strings of lights were buy one, get two free, plastic skulls were five for three bucks. I even got a spaghetti scooper/brain gouger in the shape of a witch's craggily old hand for fifty cents. I do love a deal. The lady behind the counter wished me happy holidays, to which I cheerfully answered, "And a Happy Halloween to *you!*"

I was downright fucking jolly. There were a couple of reasons for this.

First, it was Halloween again. It's so much fun to dress in someone else's life for a night, whether that be someone else's profession, or a zombie version of that. It's also nice to go out and separate the genuinely creative types from the people who went and bought whatever was prepackaged and/or slutty. There is no other time of year people distinguish who they really are by being a completely different person for a night. It's fascinating.

Second, Pat.

I didn't want that to happen. But no human being is capable of interaction at that constant of a rate without developing some sort of attachment. While laying out my costume I was nagged by a few questions that percolated up from somewhere in my guts. Would I be attached at all if he wasn't shipping out in a few days? Would I have let it go this far in the first place? Would I even have saved him from the eager beaver in the bar a few nights prior if I'd known I'd be a little crazy about him? Probably not, to all questions. It made me sad and relieved me all at once.

I decorated accordingly, filled the skulls with mini-chocolate bars as an appetizer, made a big pasta salad and served it in an authentic plastic cauldron. Candles were lit. "Werewolves of London" and "Thriller" and other seasonal favorites streamed through my speakers as I strutted around in preparation, dancing in my get-up. I hung signs in a creepy crawly script, one on the bathroom door that read,

"WHERE YOUR DINNER RISES FROM THE DEAD."
One over the bed,

"BEWARE SMALL PENISES,

FOR YE WILL BE BEHEADED."

On the refrigerator,

"TONIGHT'S SPECIAL: CHILI CON CORONOR."

I had Guillotinis chilling on ice. I was ready to raise some seasonally inappropriate hell.

Nightfall, when murders happen, comes about 4:40pm in December, so we settled on five o'clock to meet at my place. That hour seemed to drag and I couldn't get it to come quicker no matter how hard I begged Satan. It was Saturday night, and outside cars sloshed through my street teasing me. Every time I saw lights illuminate my curtains, I raced to the window thinking Pat was pulling up, hoping he'd managed to borrow a hearse somehow, but every time I was wrong. Stupid neighbors.

The five o'clock hour came and went and there I sat, in my costume, fidgeting. Every five minutes that he was later, my costume felt that much more ridiculous to be wearing.

5:30 came. No Pat. I started on a Guillotini. Was he standing me up?

By 5:36 I'd downed the entire cocktail.

5:40. Alone in my kitchen, trying not to be seen looking out the window in the event he pulled up and saw my frantic eyes. I thought of all the Halloween clichés: ghosts, vampires, Frankenstein. Nothing scared me like rejection.

I felt fifteen again. Fifteen at my locker with my gangly build and braces, and not the Junior girl on the swim team, whose locker was right next to mine and frequently festooned with a variety of suitors who felt I was in the way when I came for my Biology text. "Beat it, Railroad Tracks. You're blocking the view."

I felt eighteen again. Eighteen in my first week of college, when I couldn't start a conversation to save my life, and thus sat very alone in my dorm with a roommate, whose entire high school clique decided to come to the same university, and so had no need to latch onto me or collect me up under her wing. And so alone I listened to a lot of Grateful Dead and would have been grateful to have been dead.

I felt twenty-one again. Twenty-one on my birthday, a very forced occasion when you're expected to swing from the chandeliers. The only exception to this rule is when you show up to your own birthday "party," and one other person is standing there looking apologetic, and there isn't even a fucking cake.

I felt twenty-two again, and twenty-three, and twenty-four. Twenty-something, when he stops calling and I see him out and about, and I wrestle with asking him "Why? Fucking why?" versus preserving my dignity and acting like I'd been too busy to notice any cold shoulder.

There are plenty of déjà vu moments in a girl's life to draw from when she's sitting in a stupid costume and her date is forty five minutes late, staring at the phone like a deaf person. Luckily I'd steeled myself years before. I'd learned to stop wondering if he was in a car wreck. Stopped wondering if maybe he'd communicated the wrong time to meet. No more soothing my ego with bullshit like "he's just intimidated by me," or "he's afraid to love me." I'd stopped speculating on the "fucking why?" and focused on the What. The What: just when you are at the point of no return and would really care if he disappeared, he disappears.

But this is life, so I blew out the gravestone shaped candles.

I unplugged the orange lights.

Disarmed the motion activated witch's cackle set to crack when anyone walked the front steps.

Took down the cobwebs from the houseplants.

Detached the post apocalyptic nuclear fallout spider from the underside of the toilet seat that was set to jump out as soon as Pat took his first piss.

Six o'clock rang. I flipped on the television, grabbed the
pasta cauldron and a fork and scanned the channels. The costume
was staying on, I decided, because if there was anything sadder
than being stood up, it's sitting in my underpants and doing some
anger eating. Plus I was a little drunk.

Saturday night. *Charlie Brown Christmas* was on, which
always made me feel young and simple. Such a comfort. I numbed
myself and tried not to think of any of the previous days. They
didn't happen. Forget them. Strike them from the record. Don't let
them influence me in any way. No feelings, no lamenting what
was. Just a blank spot in my memory.

Then, because I wasn't feeling already like God had ding-
dong-ditched me, the power went out. This isn't uncommon in the
dead of winter, what with downed tree limbs and snow ruining
everything- pant legs, roadways, electricity. In the moment though,
Charlie Brown *zeerped* out just as my internal pep-talk was starting
to work. The room went black, of course after I'd blown out all the
candles, and all I could do was give up. I put my fork down and
started to cry. No, more accurately my eyes exploded. And then a
series of loud, lonely wails. Like mummy moans.

It sounded a little like this:

"Wuuuuuuuhhhhhhhhblaaaaaahhhhhhh [breath]
pubpubpubpubpubpubaggggggghhhhhhh [breath]
huhuhuhuhuhuhuhuhuhuhuhhhgahhhhh [breath] kill me…" It went
on a little longer, but you get the gist.

Pathetic.

Then a knock at the door. "Fuck," I whispered. "Nancy."
Of course she would be knocking to talk about the outage, which I
never understood why she did that. What's the point in confirming
I had no power? She could clearly look outside and see street
lamps weren't on and put it all together: electrico no happeningo.
What did she need to me to confirm for her? That the situation was
shitty? I sat as still as possible. Quiet. I tried willing it with my
mind, shutting my eyes nice and tight and putting the fork back in
my mouth so I wouldn't accidentally yell "Go home to your hole,
Nancy!"

Then I realized there was no way I could deny her if I'd
just been crying at a volume that penetrated walls, time, space, and
the walls outside of space. I cried so dramatically, the future could
hear it. There was no way I was going to convince her I was fine,
much less not home. Dammit. I was never getting rid of her.

I got to the door, making sure to take off my headpiece
before answering so as not to confuse the hell out of her, thereby

provoking more questions from her, and thus more conversation and thus a night with Nancy on my couch, being present in my life when I wanted for once to feel more sorry for myself than her. I opened it swiftly, letting the air hit my bare shoulders and blowing my hair back. "Hey, Nance…" But she wasn't there. Just the plastic jack-o-lantern I'd forgotten to bring inside. I looked left and right. No Nancy. No Michael. Honorico had not knocked either. Her car wasn't even in the driveway.

I checked my mailbox and doorknob for Mormon missionary magazines, but no. No children of God had popped by this snowy evening. I admitted to myself I wished Pat was standing there instead, wet, covered in gasoline and soot, panting, telling a harrowing story of barely escaping a pump explosion at the local service station, and he's so sorry to have kept me waiting, and my, how pretty I look, and is there any dinner left? This did not happen though.

I shut the door and rested my forehead against it. I sighed and felt the icy streaks of my recent breakdown tighten around my cheeks.

Then, like in every self defense class I took in college, the attacker came out of nowhere. I didn't so much as sense a presence much less hear him coming behind me. But there he was before I could react, bearish arms locked around me, wrapped so that I could neither scream for help nor use my limbs from the elbows down. We were taught in class to use anything and everything as a weapon, that you don't need to own a gun to protect yourself and there are plenty of other implements to drive into your attacker's eye. Throw a shoe at him, jab a pen in his ear, strangle him with a kitchen towel, squirt mildew remover in his face, whatever is handy.

But you can't be handy if you have no hands, so I could only count on my legs to save me. I wiggled and the attacker mirrored my wiggle, jerking left and right wildly. I used every muscle in my back and kicked my legs up and onto the door, then pushed back like an Olympic swimmer coming off the wall, using all the force in my body to throw us both back behind us. He slammed up against the wall and broke his grip, dropping me from his hulkish embrace so I could run for my life.

I'm kind of an idiot sometimes, so instead of running out from the front door and screaming bloody murder, I ran to the kitchen and grabbed the first thing I could get my hands on, a stainless steel colander. I guess I wanted to strain the killer to death. The psycho was on my heels, so I swung around and walloped him in the face, a loud gong coming off him and echoing around the room. He was stunned for a moment, so I took full advantage of the head start and got to my knives, which happened to be the infommercial sort that can cut right through a tennis shoe without needing to saw at it. Great when you're butchering a steak, bad when you're chopping a slippery onion. I have scars.

I already had a line ready. "I will slice and dice your ass, Dale." I said this with conviction. I would have killed him. No hesitation. I was ready. If he so much as sneezed I was prepared to lunge at him and drive that knife into everything that was meaty on him. I almost wanted to, I was so brimming with fury. Fury Nancy wouldn't let herself succumb to, fury for every ounce of disappointment I was burying, fury that anyone dare step into my home and violate the only place in the world I am truly off guard, and take my one retreat from me. I wanted revenge on it all. I wanted blood.

"Marin. Whoa. Whoa, there."

This wasn't Dale. I was shaking.

"Pat? What the fuck?!" My voice quivered and I choked.

I couldn't see all of him, just his silhouette in the little bit of moonlight coming in from the kitchen window, flickering as it bounced off my giant shoe cutter knife, which was trembling in my grasp. He reached out his hands like he was trying to approach a rabid pit bull.

"Take it easy. I was just messing." He sounded like he was smiling. I was not.

"Messing? Messing, you ass fucker?" He took a couple of steps toward me. I did not set the knife down, so he took it from me gently and set it on the counter. He tried to hug me, but I was filled with hate, so he hugged my unrelenting rigidity instead. "You think that's funny?"

"It's Halloween," he reasoned, swaying me this way and that to calm me. "You know? Trick or treat?"

"I was seriously going to kill you."

"I realize that now. I'm sorry."

"What if I'd shot you?"

"You don't own a gun. You have a glue gun."

"Those things get hot."

He laughed. I did not. "You're right. I'm sorry I scared you."

"And you're late."

He pulled back my face and angled it toward the dim light coming in from the kitchen window. "Is that why you were crying?"

"Answer the question."

"You didn't ask me a question."

I pushed him away. "Why were you late?" I went to the junk drawer and found the matches I'd used to light the candles earlier and took to lighting them all over again. Angrily.

"To build the suspense."

I handed him a lantern with a candle the shape of a femur on the inside. "And you cut my electricity?"

"No, I didn't cut all the power in the neighborhood as a joke. I'm not that good. That was just coincidence working in my favor."

"Fuck you, you know that? Fuck you."

I lit everything I could in the house. He remained quiet, waiting for me to compose myself. Everything glowed, except of course the orange lights, which I'd cleaned the drug store out of for no reason. It's only a good deal if you actually use them.

I found my headpiece and stared down at it. Pat stood across the room with his lantern, watching me.

"What are you supposed to be?"

I put on the bright red devil horns. The rest of me was twinkling in a blue sequined tube dress. Pat wasn't even wearing a costume, and I was in my living room looking like a discount hooker. "You don't know?"

"Tina Turner?"

First pissed off. "No, not Tina Turner. I'm a devil with a blue dress on." Then docile. "Get it?"

He smiled, and his face glowed in the candle light. "I like it."

"Fuck off."

He laughed.

"You couldn't even dress up?"

"I'm dressed as a rapist."

"That's not funny," but he heard my smile crack and it was all over for me. He approached me from behind, this time not like an assailant. This time he wrapped his big warm body around me and buried his face in the cul de sac between my neck and shoulder.

"Thank you for giving me Halloween."

"Yeah," I snarled.

"The place looks beautiful." He kissed my neck mole.

"I had a spider inside the toilet. It was supposed to scare the shit out of you. Get it?"

"I'm sorry."

"I had cobwebs everywhere." He nodded. "And I ate your dinner."

"That's what I get for being late."

We stayed there a minute too long, when his sweet apology turned into my hyperawareness. What we were doing, the quiet spooned embrace, was something couples did. Single guys apologize to keep the peace, because they're nice guys. Committed, monogamous guys apologize because it's easier than fighting with their girlfriends. It's an investment. Which one was this?

We were somewhere in the middle there, leaning toward the latter. It was aptly creepy. And the end was near. In a few days my unboyfriend would break up with me. Our untethered, free love sort of romance would become even more of a mind fuck. I didn't know what we were, but we certainly weren't what we set out to be.

An hour and a few kisses down the slope of my shoulder later, we were steaming bodies coming up off the living room floor. We did it with the devil horns on, his preference. I could barely see his face in the dim room. We'd had presence of mind to put our lanterns up and safely away from our flailing legs and tossed clothing. This was probably for the best, as the scene was already more exposure than I'd originally bargained for.

We laid there naked in the shadow of the Christmas tree, who looked ridiculous without lights. The room seemed quieter without the tree at attention, the unspoken things bouncing off the walls like sonar, loud and clear. I rested my head on his shoulder and he dragged his fingertips over my back slowly.

"Tell me about your last girlfriend."

He paused. "Why would you want to know that?"

I didn't know. It's not like I could stake my claim. We were only on day four of seven. This was only necessary information for those on day four of eternity. "Tell me why you split up."

"Honestly?" I nodded. He tried to find a way to say it. I prayed for *she wasn't the one*, or *we weren't a good fit,* or *she wasn't as pretty as you.* Anything but what *honestly?* is generally leading to. "I cheated on her." Yep. There it was.

I tried not to judge. It's not as though I'd never cheated. It's what my people do. But I did anyway. "Why would you do that to her?" I didn't know her. I hated her, but I also felt responsible for her, this nameless, faceless figure in my mind, whose entire identity I'd developed using my own imagination and everything I'd ever not wanted my hypothetical competition to be. Beautiful, intelligent, enigmatic, huge titted. She was my enemy, but then she was also every woman. She was me.

"I don't know." He seemed regretful, not for cheating, but for having answered my question. I couldn't blame him.

"How many of your girlfriends have you cheated on?"

"This feels like a job interview."

"Come on, how many?"

"I can't wait until we get to the part where you ask what my best and worst qualities are."

I tried not to sound impatient. "It's a simple question."

"I would say perfectionism and, are you ready for this? Perfectionism. Best *and* worst quality. Do I get the job?"

I waited for that to pass, the compulsive deflection, then tried again. "Look, you've already gotten sex from me, so there's nothing to lose. No reason not to be honest. And we're not committed, so it's not like I have to worry about you doing that to me." It hurt saying those things out loud. Sometimes you talk your thoughts, and then you remember why they were just thoughts a second ago.

"Okay, that's all true. But I still don't want you to think I'm a dick."

"Oh, God," I groaned, straddling him so he had no choice but to face me. "You cheated on all of them, didn't you?"

"No, no."

"You dirtbag. You break hearts for sport."

He smiled and stroked my sides. "Not at all. There were just a couple." Personally, I'd cheated four times in three years, or rather with four people several times each over three years. I felt him looking at me. I hoped he couldn't see inside my brain.

"Seriously. Why do you think you did it? To see if you could get away with it?"

He shook his head. "Not at all. I think I just knew I couldn't give them what they wanted. But I still wanted to be with them. So?" He shrugged. I could sense him squirming while keeping perfectly still. "I don't know. There's no excuse. I know that. I wanted what I wanted, and I wanted a lot. I'm a nice guy, but I'm still a guy." If that's explanation than I must have been born with a vestigial penis.

"That's pretty sad."

"What about you? You've never cheated?"

"Nope." I kissed him so that I could shut my eyes.

"Well, aren't you cool."

I nodded.

The truth is I'd slept with a coworker behind Caleb's back about two months into dating him, a guy who put his lip ring back in when he left the office, and therefore was everything Caleb wasn't. I would like to say it meant nothing. Though certainly that was my intention, I know now no one does anything without meaning, certainly not sex. There's a goal at hand at everything. We are all human beings, an industrious sort with no time to waste, and so even the most frivolous impulse has some sort of reward we're seeking. I don't know what the goal was with the coworker in the conference room, but I know afterward I felt like I had slain a dragon. And you don't feel that victorious, you don't feel *anything* if you're acting robotically, like his Teddy Ruxpin penis entered my animatronic vagina and battery operated intercourse was had.

I confessed to Jane, the wild one, that it was some of the better sex I'd ever had. She said, "Let's see how long you can keep it going before we get caught!" That's right, *we* get caught, like she was in on it, it was her bare ass on the conference table, and she was going to be the one to apologize when Caleb found a cologne-scented lip ring in my hair. This was a hobby for her. I had her full support.

I confessed to Cherie, the married one, that it was some of the better sex I'd ever had, and she said, "Gosh, Marin. It's like you're bragging about it or something. You're not supposed to be smiling." I suppose I was unintentionally. I'd divulged to them in the wrong order. She spent fifteen minutes talking about STDs alone.

I told her I'd never do it again, but I did a year later. I didn't seek anybody's blessing that time. Not out of shame. The girls would forgive me, if not personally pin me with a congratulatory medal. I didn't tell anyone because I realized a person needs to have some secrets. Secrets are much safer. Don't let your elementary school teacher fool you. Lying by omission is not lying. Omission is power. It is all you have that can't be taken from you. Everything else can be compromised. But what we choose to share versus protect is exactly what distinguishes us. It's one last special thing in our world, where everything is sold or bartered. Our desires, our self esteem, our principles. So I keep what I can just for me.

Paranoid people will tell you secrets are the opposite of fidelity. I think that's like saying fat is the opposite of smart. Secrets, infidelity, and loyalty can exist all together in one big stew. And frankly, unabating candor is pretty unappetizing by comparison. No thanks. Honesty is the blandest policy.

Still, I asked that of Pat. Naked. Me on top. No distractions, not even Christmas tree lights. Eye contact.

At that moment I wished he'd lied. I actually might have respected him more.

VIII.

Day five. Easily one of the best days of my life.

You can understand my falling in love with this guy after the Sunday he gave me. You will forgive me of my delusion. You will apologize for your prejudice. I am not so foolish. It was two hydrogens and an oxygen equals water. Pat plus me plus that Sunday equals heart shaped pupils, bluebirds, and blood coursing thick and hot.

He'd stayed the night after Halloween. He told me he'd packed a bag and the next day was a surprise but we'd better get our rest, which we didn't. I thought that meant he was getting up early to make breakfast, which honestly would have sufficed. I don't expect much from people, so pancakes are all it takes to get a tip of the hat out of me.

At seven he shook me like he was trying to push an old dead log into a river. I was resistant to say the least. Please refer to chapter one to hear my thoughts on getting up early any day, much less a Sunday morning, the Sabbath and therefore an agnostic's day free of responsibility. Ask me how I feel about getting up and moving when I open my eyes and am blinded by the gray light shining through foot long icicles dangling from the roof outside my window. In fact it's best not to get out of bed at all. Those things can be murderous to the wrong-place-wrong-time door-slamming home exiter.

Pat wasn't accepting my hoarse squeals as actual parlance. I thought they clearly translated to "Get your fucking hands off of me, Evil-Doer," but he read them as "Shake me harder and more aggressively." So he did.

"Up and Adam!"

"That phrase makes no sense!" I yelled from the top of my lungs under a pillow I had pulled down tight around my head, my last vestige of protection from this thing called Daytime.

"Am I not being clear enough, Marin? Let's go. Ass out of bed."

"Don't ask me a question and not let me answer it!" I paused, stalling for more time. Any more time. Anything. Just to lay there and breathe my way back to sleep. Then said meekly, "No, you are not being very clear."

Pat wasn't messing around. "Ten seconds and you're getting snow."

I was petulant. I clung to the pillow like a flotation device. "Get snow. See if I care."

"Marin, I'll do it."

"You think I'm scared of you?"

"You should be, because I don't bluff."

"Do it, asshole."

But he called *my* bluff and got up off me like a bullet from a gun. One heavy foot on the hardwood floor pointing in the general direction of the back door and a subsequent handful of snow, and I erected to a perfect ninety degree angle at somewhere in the range of six G's. I was dizzy. My hair was sideways. I was naked, and a vision.

I yawned. Eyes shut. Boobs out. Groan.

"You are completely unfuckable right now." I was.

I flipped him off and hopped out of bed, shoving him out of the way like a bull goring a matador. The bull slammed the bathroom door and groomed herself privately. I vowed to wait an hour before he was getting a smile out of me.

I stood there in my underpants, brushing my teeth, staring at my thighs. I kind of liked them that day. Shapely, feminine thighs, made to be grabbed and suckled.

On the other side of the door I heard him fussing around, I assumed making the bed. I did not come out to help him, mostly because I wasn't sure I knew how to make a bed considering I couldn't remember the last time I'd done it. Maybe sometime around my eighth grade graduation when Grandma was visiting and my mom told me to so it appeared we lived like television show families, and any time I'd ever purchased new bedding since. Fitted sheets were like wrestling a greased pig, so any effort beyond that seemed superfluous in a room made for pleasure and relaxation.

"Where we going?" I hollered through the door and my foamy face.

"I told you. It's a surprise."

"Well, I'm going to need to know what to wear."

"That's true." But then he said nothing. I stood there holding the toothbrush in mid air, like I would miss the big reveal if I kept scrubbing.

"Well?!"

"Well, what?"

I spit my mouthful out in a hurry to give him a whole other mouthful. "What the hell am I supposed to be wearing?" I flung open the door, ready to bitch, hair still sideways, boobs still bare, flaming daggers where my crusty morning eyes should have been.

But there he was before me, standing with an unflattering stay-puff parka with a Green Bay Packers logo on the right breast. "Wear your game face." He was triumphant, and we hadn't even left the house yet.

I tried to breathe. "We're going?"

He nodded, raising his palm up high. "To Lambeau." I slapped it five, hard.

"Today?" I tried to keep my cool, but imagine horizontal hair, boobs, and that look on a dog's face when you've taken him off the leash in a field full of squirrels. I hopped into his arms, wrapped my legs around his waist. He loved it.

"I know a guy. Eleven rows behind the bench. Merry Christmas."

"I'm going to pee!" I yelled into his ear.

"I know," he said, rocking me, "me, too."

An hour later we were on the road.

It's not the most comfortable drive when the amount of apparel you're wearing moves you into a higher weight class. If we had flown to the game we would have had to pay for two extra seats, this is how much of our mass wasn't actual human being. I'd been to Lambeau Field before, the Mecca for any born and bred Wisconsinite, however never in this weather, never with snow on the ground. When you're leaving the comfort of your own home and vehicle to venture into the cold white North, where you have little to save you from the bitter temperature but beer and however many farts you can squeeze into your cocoon of protective clothing, well, it is essential to over-prepare.

What does it mean to over-prepare? Imagine the planning and process of getting into this moon suit: two pairs special winter socks made of material not found on Earth, underneath traditional snow boots with faux fur lining guaranteeing warmth in temperatures all the way down to negative ten degrees, which in laymen terms is the temperature you know you're in when your vagina completely seals shut so that even if you're dead, your eggs can still be salvaged and harvested in a foreign womb. Tucked into these clunky boots were my favorite thermal underwear, which is the color and texture of neck to ankle microwave waffles, which I ask you to suspend judgment of, referring back to the vacuum sealed vagina we in these parts are familiar with. Over that, thick stirrup stretch pants that were a touch too big, and when I say "a touch," I mean they came up over my gut so that the thick elastic band left a semi-permanent railroad track pattern just under my boobs. I realize these are maternity pants, but I recommend them as a layer no matter what your gestational condition. Then my bib overall ski pants, which remove any semblance of hourglass shape you're lucky enough to have been blessed with, as well as any semblance of sensuality, as well as any semblance of gender. Long sleeved Packers tee, hooded Packers sweatshirt, aforementioned Packers parka, green fuzzy muffs for my ears, a plush ring to go around my neck and over my mouth during painful blusters from Old Man Winter, and a bold yellow knit hat with fluffy pompon off the top that I'd been wearing since I was in high school and was attached to the way little ones cling to their blankie. And of course Iceland approved gloves that cancelled out any hopes for dexterity, good luck with that zipper, but protected well enough I could pluck flaming hot coals right out of a tailgate grill.

It took seventeen minutes to get dressed.

But this is all part of the fun. True, it's also a little miserable. You have three feet of padding between you and the aluminum bench beneath your ass, but little by little the cold metal seeps up into your tailbone and suddenly you can't move your knees. You do what you can, shove hand warmers down your shorts, piss yourself, but you're never, ever quite comfortable. All around you steam rises off unidentifiable blobs in green and yellow and blaze orange hunter's gear, and in a quiet camaraderie you are in it together. No one comments on the weather, it isn't necessary. No one complains about anything but bad calls. No one says "When are they going to put a dome on this place?" because that would remove the pride of fortitude that simply being a fan awards us. Other teams heat their stadiums and serve salads at concession stands, and people are seen on the big screen eating ice cream cones in December. By contrast, Lambeau treats us like shit and refuses to modernize beyond repaving the parking lot, and that is what separates us. We are animals. We dare you to play in this uninhabitable land called Green Bay, where you might come home with all your digits intact. Our players don't even wear gloves, but our opponents lose sensation in their faces three minutes into the first quarter. And we in the stands are there, too, and we aren't bitching. It is a painful experience. It is magical.

But I'm getting ahead of myself. Tailgating should preclude all sporting events, if there is any harmony in the world, where your vehicle gets to know the passengers of your neighbors', where you lend hot sauce to the guy who introduces himself but is essentially an anonymous frozen red nose peeking through the four inches of exposure his head gear has afforded him. We all know what we need to know of each other based off whatever music is broadcast from our parking spots, how elaborate our cooking stations are, who's grilling walleye they caught themselves from a hole in the ice, whose truck is the biggest, who's drunkest, who has the most hilarious get-up, because there's always someone in green body paint and not much else. These things are really all you need to know about a person. They are enough detail to provide a psychological profile, but not enough to make anyone uncomfortable. For instance the guy in the big truck has masculinity issues, but I know nothing of his latent homosexuality.

Pat and I and our puffy disguises grilled bratwurst and tried to eat potato chips with our big mitts, dropping more in the trodden snow than we got in our mouths. I ate two brats just to feel the heat of them defrost my snot, chewing and swallowing as quickly as possible so as to burn my esophagus raw. Pat laughed when the ketchup exploded onto my pants and I didn't even bother wiping it up. It would freeze and flick off in a minute or two anyway. He seemed proud.

During the game we shared spirits from a flask with a father and his teenaged son sitting next to us. Dad called it cruel and unusual to bring a kid in December and deny him the relief of bourbon. I suppose I agree. There was no youthful rebellion on the kid's part, he was just trying to survive. I complimented him on his sunglasses, which had green and yellow LED lights racing around the frames in a figure eight path. At the end of the game the kid gave them to me, and his dad patted him on the back for such a gesture.

At halftime we took the time to straighten our joints, maneuver out of our suits to pee, then climb back into them, then buy more beer to pour directly into the swollen and sore bladders we had just emptied out. It was a cycle that would continue endlessly and with greater frequency for the rest of the day, as that first piss seems to weaken the urethra, once a levee, now a coffee filter. We sat back in our seats after halftime and took a moment just for us, when our benchmates were still fighting their way back. Pat and I shared nachos, which is to say I ate three chips and one jalapeno, and the rest disappeared into his face as though being vacuumed directly into his stomach. I called his mouth a "nach-hose" for the rest of the day, which got funnier the more I said it.

Pat came out of nowhere with a little of his history. "I always thought I would be a pro football player."

"Didn't every little boy?" Certainly every girl has heard a guy recount the glory of his eleventh grade touchdown as though it was nationally televised, and we as women pretend to be impressed.

"Yeah, but I was pretty serious. Totally obsessed."

"Were you any good?" Lava in the form of cheese remnants burned the roof of my mouth.

"Yep. Was scouted and everything."

"No shit. Which position?" My tongue wandered to that little charred skin flap that nacho cheese is notorious for.

"Running back."

"What happened?"

He paused, looking out to the field like those memories exhausted him. I wove an arm into his and tried to feel anything solid underneath the parka. "The Army happened," he answered, very matter of fact, zero emotion.

"You gave up your lifelong dream for the military?" He didn't answer me. He gave his nacho his undivided attention. "That's ridiculous."

"It isn't for anyone to understand but me," and he meant it.

I could assume why Pat enlisted. I had put it all together by that point anyway. Just the night before he told me he signed up January 2002, his senior year of high school, and a good year for recruiters, historically speaking. One could walk blindfolded through his cafeteria and spot a patriot willing to die for his country, that year anyway. Pat was young, full of a naïve sense of destiny, as though any eighteen year old understands the difference between destiny and a craving for purpose, but he was old enough to sign the documents. All the elements were there, and so he gave it all up, going from player to spectator.

"Maybe you're better off. I don't think I could ever be a pro athlete." True statement, except for the part about him being better off.

"Let me guess. Too violent?" I hated when he talked to me like I was some prissy girl.

"No, I like the violence part. It's just that it's too disappointing. There can only be one winner every year, and the odds of that being you are so slim. It's like a kick in the nuts every year. And then, suppose you're grand champion and you're on cereal boxes, you can never just win and then be a winner forever. You have to start over every year, like you didn't just win the Superbowl last year, and if you do everyone hates you for it. If you're a champion every year, people start criticizing you for being overpaid, and everyone gets bored of you, even though you've done nothing but be really good at your job. But most of the time you're not going to be a champion every year, and so even if you do win, you know in the back of your mind you can only celebrate a few months, because no one is going to care next season. A win isn't even a win."

Pat put a nacho down and stared at me like it just dawned on him I was crazy. "Wow. You really have a way of overthinking things."

"Fine, but it's all true. It's disappointing."

"Well, I have news for you, Marin. That's called life. That's why people use sports metaphors for every life lesson. Take the ball and run, three strikes and you're out, and all that."

"Whatever."

"Well, what's the alternative?" He seemed a tad incensed. "Win the Superbowl at twenty-five years old and retire? Or stop holding Superbowls?"

"I'm not saying the system is flawed. There should be a Superbowl every year. I'm just saying I couldn't do it. There's so little glory after having worked so hard."

He shook his head and took a bite. "Okay, so take football out of it. Isn't that the case no matter which career you're in? You can't be number one forever. And you wouldn't want to be. Even if we're talking about a brain surgeon, it's not like he's going to want one successful brain transplant in his life. I would argue we *like* to start over. It's human nature."

Father and son sat back down next to us with four arms worth of concessions. We all gave the chin nods and went about our philosophical discussion.

"I guess I'm not human then."

Pat was frustrated. "That's your insecurity talking."

"Moi?" I shirked.

"Yeah," fired up, "if you want one win and no one else can win after you, that's all ego talking. But if you accept starting over as a part of life, that means you're in it to become a better person. You accept challenge as part of growth. No challenge, no growth." I knew it. He *was* the quiet ruler among his friends. His Army buddies must have looked to him like the big brother they always wanted. "Jesus, you've never heard that it's about the journey, not the destination?" He was right. I still shook my head and distorted my face so as to indicate he was full of shit though, as is my way.

He had some valid points. Instead of saying so aloud, I tried finding someone in a goofy outfit so we could change the subject. A die-hard fan in a green loin cloth, the guy we saw in the parking lot who looked just like Vince Lombardi, the heavy-set woman in skin tight shiny green leggings who fell down while descending to her seat and stood up without having spilled a drop of her beer. Where were these people when I needed a diversion? For the first time we were surrounded only by a sea of nondescript lumps.

"You don't even realize who you are," he said to me, like this should bother me. And he was right, so it did.

I know this should have been a bitter moment, when I was judged by Pat. I could have rolled his analysis into a ball and tossed it out as maliciously intended and refuse to even consider it. But he was right. I love the ups and downs, everyone does. Everyone must, or there would be no evening news. I must, or else I would never have sabotaged my past relationships, would never have switched majors four times, or paid off my credit card and then went out the next day and bought a pair of boots that came under my credit limit by six dollars. I will pay off the boots in roughly a hundred and seventy-five years, and every payment made will break my heart, for the leather split on the seam six months after the purchase, and they sit in a corner of my closet like I just can't bring myself to take them off life support. I knew this risk when I bought the boots, that I would suffer one day. I knew the pain I was putting myself in, and yet I indulged for six months of fleeting fashion joy.

As it turns out, I am human after all, which is very
disconcerting.

But the mood shifted when the Packers won in a white-
knuckler by one point, the field goal of divine providence throwing
the crowd into a jamboree of noise makers, cow bells, drums, air
horns, and squeals of all ages. Strangers hugged, even I did, ice
queen sitting in her ice bowl, thankful for all the layers protecting
me from the weird boob mash. I chest-bumped a security guy. I
thought about calling my mom. I was overcome with cheer. My
ribs hurt from the tension of those last few moments, as well as a
day's worth of weather being sucked in and out of my lungs. Pat
rested his forehead against mine and smiled, and I knew that would
be a moment he would remember and keep for himself like a
weathered photo tucked deep in his wallet. Though he technically
gave that day to me, I like to think I gave a little bit back to him.

The blackest of nights travelled with us away from the
stadium. An hour out of town and all that was lit were taillights,
the glow of the dashboard, and a zillion white pin points that
winked hello to me from galaxies beyond as I leaned my face up
against the passenger side window. I felt very alone with him on
that long stretch of nowhere, more than any night spent in bed
together. We drove in silence, except for his yawns. My body
worked so hard all day to be warm, by then even my veins were

weak. My head hurt, my skin burned, my knees, hips, and ankles were all locked in place, and my heart, though it barely beat to keep me alive, beamed like a Red Giant from inside my chest, winking back up to the stars.

IX.

Day six. Frankie and Annette hit the beach.

In winter the beach is frozen over, and the sand underneath first crystallizes, then snow fills in all the cracks like water to concrete dust. From a distance it looks soft, like one could roll down a hill of snow and be swallowed right up under it. But up close it is a solid, stubborn slab.

May as well play on it.

Most people on Christmas Eve spend the day wrapping presents or being together or going to church or whatever else is saved for one day of the year. We were free of that burden because of our arrangement, and though we were nearing the end, I was enjoying the flexibility of being in love with someone for only two more days. When you know it's going to be over soon, you don't waste too much time on petty jealousy, or the more generic "issues." Maybe this is the secret to a good relationship.

Acknowledge it is perishable and know the date on the milk carton. Maybe a good relationship is good precisely because it is temporary. Maybe the expectations of forever are exactly what drive people to mistreat one another, creating a black hole sort of power mongering, sucking all sense of delight down into oblivion, until no one in the relationship even wants to be in love anymore, they just want to win and outlast each other. And maybe I shouldn't quit my day job to write greeting cards.

But here we were, our delight spilleth over. That morning I suggested to Pat we suit up again and traverse the city with hot coffees and the spirit of our youth. He agreed. As adults we don't make time to do these things unless we are trying to entertain children. This might be why people have kids in the first place, to feel the way they once had before social pressures crept in along with all the people who disillusion us into being suspicious of each other. Perhaps children fulfill our innate desire to be indiscreet, to swing naked from the rafters singing off-key from the pits of our diaphragms with all the trust in the world that there is a corps of people waiting with arms outstretched to catch us should we fall. We long for an imprudent existence, which we tend to lose right about the time we are of the age to watch network television and its insidious commercials. On the sly they tell us we're not good enough, and our lives crumble a little more every year until death.

Age six, give or take. This is when our lives start to end. Happy birthday. You're dying.

About a third of the way through this lifetime though, Pat and I unconsciously recaptured that recklessness by renting a couple pairs of cross country skis and poles. During summer I typically rent canoes from the same guy, so it was comforting to see he had income during gift giving season, too.

Neither of us had tried the sport before. The closest I ever came was when I fell off Caleb's elliptical machine not too long before. He chastised me for using it wrong while I rubbed my shin and writhed. I told him no real man owns an elliptical. We called it even and I agreed never to go near the thing again.

So here Pat and I were on the beach of Lake Michigan watching slushy waves rock in and out in slow motion like gelatin setting, gliding along clumsily in our skis. We looked like total idiots. He, a natural athlete, had no sense for the coordination it took to know just when to push that back leg forward so that the front leg met it halfway so as to propel him ahead. Instead he moved with the smooth grace of a robot, if he moved at all, his skis shuffling in place for the most part, like a cartoon animal running in mid-air just off the edge of a cliff.

I was worse. At least he had the stamina to keep trying and improve incrementally as the two hours of rental time elapsed. I apparently should not have relied on all the sex we'd been having to maintain my lower body agility and muscle tone. If I could get my arms and legs to move at all in the rhythm they were supposed to, my quads and hammies were like hollowed out tree trunks and possessed as much horse power as an overfed housecat. Three strokes, hands on knees, pant for my life, repeat. This was the cycle.

Still had fun anyway. There aren't a lot of people who would spend Christmas Eve that way, or any day that way. It is much easier in that weather to lay in soft, oversized clothing on a sofa eating hot food and competing for Most Drowsy. With him, all alone in the tundra, I was safe to make a fool out of myself and try something I knew from the outset would not be one of my hidden talents. We would not have discovered my God given cross country skill under any circumstances, but this was still fine by me.

Eventually I was sweating more than I was freezing, which I know was supposed to be the objective. But without any sort of payoff of having achieved anything, no medal at stake, filthy pits get old quick. Luckily we were on the same page. From yonder Pat waved his pole in the air and then crossed them like a "T" overhead, yelling "Time!" at me from his distance.

"Thank God," I said to God, looking right up at him. I stepped out of my skis and onto the beach. He did the same and ran as best he could through heavy breathing and the cumbersome equipment he was holding over his shoulder.

"Land!" he announced once he reached me. "I would get down and kiss it if my back wasn't spasming."

"That was awesome. Let's get the hell out of here."

He agreed. This was fun, but it was no day at the beach.

A bit later we returned our skis. As the gentleman behind the counter handed me the receipt he said to me, "It's nice to see you in the off season."

I was touched, replied, "I was hoping you would remember me. Merry Christmas," and stuck my hand out for him to shake it.

He did, and said, "Usually you're alone. It's nice to see you with a boyfriend for once." *I rescind my "Merry Christmas," sir.*

How embarrassing. Must he have added "for once" at the end there? I wanted to tell him I'd had Caleb all the while, that I wasn't a loser, and in fact I'd dumped *him* callously, at the supermarket in front of strangers on the eve of an important national holiday, and therefore that makes me a heartbreaker and not a "for once" kind of girl, thank you very much. It's just that I didn't like to take Caleb to my happy place, where I fumbled with my canoe paddles and got just about nowhere with them, and that was fine so long as I was alone. I wasn't going to take Caleb anywhere that I could be subjected to his instruction. I didn't need to feel inferior to someone like him.

But I didn't correct the guy. Too good of a mood.

Afterward Pat and I sat in his truck and looked over the lake with our seats scooted back and our feet on the dash. The engine was running and the heat was on, but still we huddled under a blanket. Beyond us the horizon blurred into the lake like ombre paint. The longer I stared at all that white I lost my depth perception. I was in the vehicle, I knew I was in the vehicle, but my vision cancelled out everything around the fringe so that I floated right out over the sea, sucked out and away like an atmospheric rip tide. I smudged into the landscape like there was no distinct me anymore, like I was no longer tied to my body and was just a dream-state me asking myself "am I awake?" even though no one awake ever asks herself that question. Winter and fatigue and the company of each other made us drift to a quiet consciousness. A few months later and this water would be teeming with birds and wayward Frisbees, the scent of fake coconut and flirtation in the air, distractions abound, where I couldn't soak into the horizon if I tried.

Pat reached over and rested his arm on mine, grazing his knuckles over my arm hair so that I got a chill, and shivered awake to the here and now.

"I was somewhere else for a second there," I said in that oozy kind of way that happens when you're dozing off.

I was hungry but didn't want to move my body. I could tell he was looking at me by the feel of the air space in the front cab of the truck, like he had moved into one of my wavelengths and I was feeling the weight of him tug on me. "What'cha thinking?" I asked, not looking back at him, figuring he wouldn't be staring at me if he didn't have something to say.

He breathed in deep. "Let's have sex."

Like a direct current to my vagina I awakened from the midsection up, bolting forward with such a force it even shocked me. First a dizzy haze, then perfectly alert, zero to sixty in whatever time it takes for endorphins to rush through my blood like they're fighting their way through all my valves and detours to get to my nipples, lips, and all those other things that are supposed to swell up when a good looking boy says words like those. Worse, when I met his gaze an uncontrollable grin took over my face, cracking it wide open so that when I clamored over the center console to get to him, all he saw were tonsils and teeth, tongue like a flag at full staff. He laughed as I straddled as best I could, digging my leg into that impossibly narrow spot where the seat belt clicker is rooted, the other hanging on for dear life between the seat and the door, my feet clunking around the steering wheel so that the turn signals and windshield wipers never were the same any day after, never quite thunking into place like they had originally. We kissed like we were running out of time, breathing into each other from down deep in our bellies the anguish of why we were there and what it would all mean in two days. He could barely feel me over all my layers, but already I was communicating in short grunts in an octave I typically reserved for drunk sex only, I suppose because I always felt drunk with him. I pressed what I could against him through our clothes, then realized I would have to take it all off if any of this was going to work properly.

I know no one should be thinking the word "properly" when having raw, animal sex in a very public state-owned beach parking lot. But vehicle sex in general requires a fair amount of knowledge of geometry and one's own capacity for bending and flexing in a way human anatomy is not built for. Darwin is sitting up there, in heaven ironically enough, watching and waiting for us to evolve away from a primate body style to something much more conducive to dirty one-night stands with someone whose last name we know in 40% of such escapades. In short, vehicle sex is tricky to pull off, much less enjoy.

I would like to say I slithered back over to my side and sexily removed my clothes like a Parisian burlesque dancer, with a pout and lick of the top lip, but I am me and not that person. It is fair to say I exist as that person's polar opposite so as to balance the universe somehow. I have guts, and I am sexual, but I do not operate with cat-like ease with boys like Pat, which I hope is part of my charm. Rather, I exited his lap less like a cat and more like canned bread dough being squeezed out onto a cookie sheet into a shapeless dump of beige glop. Again, I lobby on behalf my charm.

Further, when you're trying to get to someone's penis in a rush, the clothes you're wearing never seem to end. Every garment feels like peeling away a strip of wallpaper and finding no one bothered to take off the last one, and son of a bitch, how long was this one going to take to rip off, and motherfucker, a *third* layer of wallpaper?! I could feel his impatience as he yanked at my sleeve to help, but he was only getting in the way, so I swatted him violently, "Let me do this," then became aware that was a mood killer and leaned over and grabbed his face. "I'm sorry," I said through hard kisses.

"It's okay, just take off your God damned pants."

Off they came and into a pile and I don't even remember the leap over to his lap. I was suddenly on him before I knew I'd even left the passenger seat, like a version of me was just floating over the lake still, sitting over there saying, "Hey, what about me?" She jumped back into my body and we were all in it together then, my face smushed on his, because if I sat straight up my head hit the roof of the truck. As unerotic as any of this was, the last thing I needed was to add a craned neck and hunchback. He was not there to fuck Igor.

The truck filled with the giggles and sweet foibles of amateur love making, like this was the only private place in the world for our seemingly inexperienced hands to explore each other, in this, the only parked automobile within a mile, that at the moment was rocking in a conspicuous way, but thank Jesus was never disturbed by a state trooper. I screamed like this was my first taste of freedom, since that's exactly what it felt like and was the only sex I'd ever had in my life that wasn't tainted by his insecurity or a lingering possession of the girl who came before me and told him of his flaws related or unrelated to his sexual mastery, which he wore like a greasy film when his clothes were off. This was not that, as I'd known sex before. This was risk free. He had no qualms about my physique or whether I was the best of his bevy of lays, and neither did I, and so like a couple of awkward donkeys we managed to get through the illegal act with a couple of chipped toenails, sweat rings frizzing our hairlines, and bruises my mother would be worried for and suggest I "get checked out," as she used to say after some of my more brutal one-on-ones in seventh grade basketball.

Afterward we laughed but said nothing. I stayed in his lap while he stared at me, and I listened to the wonders circulate through his brain, felt the sear of his eyes as they moved along the ridges of my face. Then I realized he could see me staring, too, and maybe he was just wondering what I was wondering.

My legs were weak and worthless after that feat. The passenger seat was way over there, and I didn't know if I could make it on my own. I felt like a newborn deer, everything shook. "Can you give me a shove?" I asked. Pat dislodged my foot from the driver side door cavity and, carrying 85% of my weight, practically picked me up and vaulted me over. I landed in a pa-clump. "You clearly weren't on top. I'm spent."

"It was nice to be serviced for once," he smirked.

I rolled my eyes.

He flopped the blanket over me to protect my bare genitals from the cold and potentially peeping cops. I reclined my seat all the way back and curled my legs up so that I was all snuggles and satisfied *mmmmmmmm*s. Pat revved the engine to pump warmer air into the cab, and I reached my hand to his forearm in appreciation.

"You want to go?" he asked me softly.

"Go where?"

"Home?"

"No," I was too comfortable. I liked this dream state. "A little longer. Can we?"

"It's going to get colder in here," he warned.

"Well, we can go when that happens. For now it's perfect. Everything is perfect."

Pat resigned and reclined his seat as far as it would go, turning on his side to face me. He said so casually, like it wasn't a bother on his mind, "Fantasy land is going to be over soon." He yawned. "And you're going to wonder if this even happened."

"I don't know if I'm here now."

"Yeah," he replied.

It did all feel less like I was living it and more like I was looking back on it. It felt like the now was the next day and I was zooming around in a post-coital high, trying desperately to remember every last detail so as to never lose the sensation. I could have just shut my mind off and been there with him, but instead I closed my eyes and smelled the air, pungent wafts of body fluids trapped around us and fogging the windows like they were their very own gas on the periodic table of elements. Gn, for Genitalium.

I listened to the truck hum and cough occasionally, like it was working hard but not to worry, boss, it won't let you down. I felt the vents puff lukewarm heat onto my face and dry it so that if I smiled, my young crows' feet cracked and my eyelids burned. I felt so heavy in the seat, like that position to be laying in was the angle I'd been searching for my whole life, like I hadn't been so soothed since I was a womb dweller. I begged for nothing to itch so that I could stay there forever and ever, even though in five minutes my hip would ache and my shoulder would go numb. Nothing lasts forever. But as soon as you dread an itch, that's right when one arrives.

I broke character to scratch the underside of my nose.

"I thought you were dead," Pat cooed.

"If I died right now, I'd be okay with it," I smiled, eyes shut. It was true. This is a little scary, but a glimmer of wanting to disappear happened. Soon enough all of this would be gone- the romance, the exclusivity of me to him and him to me, the fake world of kissing and sleeping in and goofy stuff, like naked arm wrestling, naked show and tells of our respective party tricks (his white guy break-dancing, my squeezing my entire fist in my mouth), naked cooking, naked eating, naked dish duty, all without ever feeling naked- all gone. He had become my best omission.

In the days spent together I managed not to tell a soul where I'd been and who I was with. It was Pat and me and a whisper in a coat closet. He could leave and I could tell anyone he happened, and no one would have any reason to believe me. It was all that absurd, knowing a man for seven days and no longer. Or I could tell no one and carry all of this with me like a scar, and everyone would see something in my face, a life lived outside their reality, but they could never guess exactly what, and I would enjoy that. They would look at me and wonder and I would blush.

It was all mine.

The secrets. I was perfectly exposed, but safe.

The sex. For once it wasn't a power struggle. It was pure.

The peace. There were no schedules or obligations or apologies or failures.

The solitude. I'd spent plenty of holidays in rooms chock full of people telling stories and asking me questions and being a big old presence. Those rooms were always so lonely. And I'd spent holidays in the past with one boyfriend or another, and I saw his interest in me and attention he gave as a violation of my personal space, and yes, that felt exceptionally lonely. Lonelier even. Now here was a person, more inside my thoughts and space in that he was a direct inhalant of my carbon dioxide, who could damage me forever with all he'd learned of me in just a short time, and I had never felt better.

How baffling to sort through though, to make it all line up in my mind in precise grids as though it was psychologically healthy. In a loopdy-loo my mind went: I could feel this good because I knew he was going away. But when I realized I felt that good, I never wanted him to leave. A win became a loss and became a win and became a loss, and on and on, until eventually I had to ask myself that if I had to analyze why I was happy, than I probably wasn't really happy at all. In short, I was fucked up inside.

And then I realized I was crying, which was humiliating.

Pat reached over and cupped the side of my head, digging his fingers in my hair, tight. "We aren't crying on Christmas Eve. It isn't allowed. Elves are watching." He didn't ask me why or try to comfort me. He simply outlawed acknowledging the facts of the matter, that this was all disintegrating by the hour.

"I'm not crying." My face was cherry red. There were clearly tears pouring out of my face rendering me blind. My lips quivered like a kid in time-out. But I stood by my story. "I just yawned."

"Okay," he didn't press.

I didn't want to talk about it. On the other hand it was squeezing out of me, like a button was going to fly off my clothes and my insides would come spilling out. I looked at him through my tear goggles. He held my head still, eyes shut, and his breathing was tense. I didn't need to say it. He was thinking it. He knew how I felt because it was shooting out the side of my head and down his arm. I didn't need to tell him how fucking confusing it all was, how it didn't seem possible to only care for someone because they were temporary. What's next? A cancer patient? Should I proactively seek out people in known dangerous careers so as to increase the likelihood there would be a clear and imminent end to us? Was I really going to be stuck with crab fishermen and high-rise window washers my whole life? What the fuck was wrong with me? Did I even love him? It sure felt like it, but did I really? Or did I just love the immediacy of him? I knew I wouldn't have any answers until Pat was gone and I was back to my big gray world where I smiled and told jokes but lived every important part of my life in my own head. None of this felt like heartbreak I'd ever felt before. It felt more like I was chasing a 747 down the tarmac, knowing the futility in it, being blasted pitifully by engine exhaust. And so I cried, this time aloud, inexorably, like this wave was breaking and there was no way I or anyone else had a right to stop it.

I dug my face down deep into the blanket. I don't know his reaction except that he held my head tighter, and I felt his own torment shoot up his arm and into my head, trading emotions through touch alone. He didn't tell me to stop, never shushed me, never handed me a hankie, possibly because they stopped making those in the 1950's, possibly because he knew what I was feeling was perfectly justifiable, even if it felt like lunacy in my own head. He waited, and held me.

And then I ruined everything. "Why did you do this?"

"Do what?"

"Why did you do this to me?"

"Do what?"

"What is this about for you?" I could barely make out what I was saying through the crying, choking, and gasps for air.

"I don't know what you're talking about." I came out from under the blanket and opened my eyes. His forehead was squeezed together like an accordion, and he seemed to be a smidge frightened of me.

"Did you want a week of sex? Is that why you asked me out?"

"You're asking if when I offered to go get you a Christmas tree if it was all a plot to sleep with you?"

I nodded.

"Well, sure. I was attracted to you. I wanted to sleep with you."

I dropped my head back down, hiding. I barked muffled assumptions. "Oh, I see. Fuck the lonely girl. Fuck her for a week and then throw her away." All of it was irrational. I knew it was. I couldn't articulate this crisis, it was all too much to sort. Some things are impossible to sort when you're standing at the edge of them, peering down into the maelstrom. I always hated jigsaw puzzles. A cornfield maze twenty miles from where I grew up gave me the sweats just driving by it. When my necklaces are tangled I spend about six seconds on them and then toss them out, no matter what I paid for them. On some tangles, no matter the amount of resilience, nothing is going to shake them loose. I always calculated the numbers, divided the amount of time by the risk of failure multiplied by the potential for success, squaring it by the dollar value of the necklace, carried the one, and then reasoned it was easier to yell "Fuck it!" and throw it in the garbage like it had offended me personally.

In the truck, with my fears and love and yearning and despair and uncertainty, I couldn't untangle it all. All stuck together, none of it made sense, so instead of taking a breath and being thoughtful in a peaceful place down deep, I shouted the opposite of what little I knew to be true. "That's what I am. I am your play thing. I am a dog toy."

"A dog toy, Marin?"

"A slobbered up tennis ball."

"A slobbered up tennis ball. Seriously? Wasn't this all your idea? I believe it was you who asked me to stay with you."

"Yes, but not for this."

"For what? Sex? You didn't want sex?"

"No!" Lie.

"Okay, so I coerced you. I see."

"Basically." Lie.

"You are shitting me."

I shook my head. "You got yours, and now you're leaving town."

He grabbed my face with both hands a bit too hard, but I wouldn't look him in the eye. "I'm not even gone, Marin. I'm sitting here with you. You can't see that? We are enjoying ourselves." He was calm but firm, and enunciated to me like I was his willful child. I broke free from him and tore off the blanket abruptly, reaching for my pants. He read me like this book and took them right out of my hands, tucking them behind his back. "You're not getting dressed."

"Really, Pat? I can't get dressed now? First you use me, now I have to be naked until you permit me to dress?" I was off the deep end by then, no logic in sight. I see it now.

"Which part of that is the craziest? Because I'll address that first."

"Give me my pants." I held out my hand as though I was intimidating enough for this to actually yield results.

"You're not going anywhere. It's twenty-five degrees out." He kept his finger near the power lock to block any attempt I made to dart out of the truck in a sweatshirt, socks, and my birthday pants.

"I hate you!"

"And I didn't use you. We were both there. Yes, I'm going away. Yes, this worked perfectly for my lifestyle. But if I used you, you used me, too."

"Your lifestyle? Easy there, Big Shot. Nobody's impressed."

He got in my face and grabbed my wrists. "I'm in the Army. Get that through your head. I live on the other side of the world, and I like it that way. I designed it that way. There will never be a you and me because I don't want it. And you may as well admit to yourself you don't either." I shook my head and tears shot out of me. "You asked *me* to spend the week with *you*. I didn't dream that."

He could have my wrists, but I couldn't stand that look in his eyes. I couldn't bear it. "Take me home."

He meant every word. I didn't know if I disagreed, I didn't care. I just knew my heart was going to convulse and die if I heard anymore.

"No."

"Take me home, Pat. I'm done with you. I throw you away. Fuck it. You're of no use to me anymore. Take me home so I can get on with my life." Passion, mania, sweat pooling all over me.

He dropped my wrists with purpose and turned to the steering wheel. "You're not you. I don't know who you are." He shifted the truck into reverse.

"Give me my pants."

"You'll get them when we're home."

"It's not your home. Don't fucking forget that. Your home is on the other side of the world. You designed it that way," I mocked.

"Yep. That's right. And thank God." Pat peeled out of the parking lot, slipping on some ice so that we fishtailed onto the main road. I cried more, and then more, and the city flew by us too quickly, like this was the fastest car ride I'd ever taken. It was all a test. I threw him away so he would call my name and tell me he loved me. I said "take me home" so he would say "no," but he didn't say that. He refused to play my game. I stared out the window pouting, as though so much as turning my head a centimeter to the left would mean defeat.

Slow down, I begged on the inside. *Slow this fucking truck down*, as landmarks flew by us like bugs dodging the windshield. He said nothing, I said nothing, and time was running out to save us, whatever the hell was left.

I wanted him to know the emotions fighting their way out of me. I wanted to say too many things, like "I love you," and "please don't go," and everything else that he could do nothing with and might freak him out. I didn't want to say them for Pat's benefit, I wanted to say them so he would say them back, even though I had no right to his love.

The universe didn't push us together for that. I know now why it did, but at the time I didn't. I just reasoned correctly that the time to shout "Stay!" is not when someone is walking away from you. We are people, not dogs.

"I love you" shouldn't be a desperate plea, especially if you're hoping it's reciprocated. Even if I did love someone, if they told me these words in this manor I would immediately fall out of love with them. Desperate pleas are boner killers.

"Please don't go" is not a scene from a train station in a romantic comedy starring the guy with the abs and the girl who is clumsy but gorgeous. If "please don't go" is being said, that right there is a pretty good red flag the person you're saying it to wants to get away from you, quickly.

I admit it though. All of this wisdom only came later. In the moment I was simply afraid, and so I kept my mouth shut.

I worried about what I would say when we pulled up to the house, but before I could come up with something profound that he would take with him all his days and pass down to his children one day, we were in the driveway, and all I had so far was a mental list of scribbles scratched out, none of them coherent or earth shattering, fits and starts of soap opera one-liners.

You can't go your whole life alone...

You can run from me, but you can't run from love...

If you can't be real with me, you'll never be real with anyone...

You are trapped in your own prison, and until you love you will never be free...

And then in my mind I puked all over that list.

Pulling into the driveway, Pat slammed on the brakes and my head jerked forward. He handed me my pants and rested the side of his face in his palm, watching me dress. He sighed. "So. We on for Christmas?"

Everything I wanted to hear, but still I just glared at him, then threw open the car door and stepped out. "Fuck Christmas!" I shouted so loudly my neighbors' wall crucifixes all crashed to the ground in protest. I hoped he would wait until I was inside, but he screeched out and away from my hysteria before I could get passed his bumper. His urgency to escape shook me, and I watched as he disappeared down the street.

Once in the door I leaned my forehead against it, remembering when he faux attacked me just a few days prior. Such a sweet memory.

I told myself things so I could sleep that night. I told myself that if he lived in town it would be tumult and public disagreements, and an addictive cycle of slammed car doors and destructive sex. I convinced myself I was too old for that. But the truth is if he lived in town and in an opportune place to be my unending tempest, we likely wouldn't even know each other, because if I knew he was permanent I never would have bothered with him in the first place.

I slept on the couch with the tree turned off, daring Santa's fat ass to come down the chimney so I could kick him right in his jolly balls.

X.

Day seven. Christmas.

It's funny, the refuge of your home, when the windows are opaque with frost, the heater blowing to beat hell, as though all the windows and doors are sealed and no one is getting in or out. It's funny because my home proved to be no protection at all from two intruders who made this the Christmas I never talk about.

First off I woke up on the couch with the same clothes on from the day before, which had twisted around my body like swirly soft serve ice cream, yanking my boobs in unnatural positions I could do nothing about in the stupor of my sleep. I hadn't brushed my teeth. I still had on my big yellow wool cap, the pompon I loved about it dangling off the arm of the couch. Frozen tears from the day before had dried and crusted onto my face. If one looked up "Broken Woman" in the dictionary, my photo would be too gruesome to display, but my name and address would be listed for specific reference to where this beast lay, in the event someone wanted to come and poke me with a stick. In short, I looked, felt, and smelled like shit.

While I was dreaming I settled on a plan of taking a bunch of nighttime cold medicine every time my stupid brain got done sleeping and wanted to wake up. That way I could snooze right through Christmas and wake up sometime after I knew Pat was in the air and on his way to his drought ridden hell hole across the globe. I figured the only way to win was to be so asleep I couldn't even feel apathy for him. I would feel nothing about anything.

This was not an option available to me however, since I woke up to Pat shoving a snowball down my pants. I tried to leap out of my skin but the full weight of him kept me pinned, and the snow smushed right up against my ass and thighs, oozing down into my crack and the narrow divide of my legs. I didn't say a word. I just groaned and lurched, waiting for the cold to turn to numb so he would be satisfied with how hilarious he thought he was.

His body shifted so that his face was down now, breathing into the back of my ear and pressing my face flat against the side of the couch, my pucker jutting like a kid with too many braces in her mouth. I felt all of him on me, and I loved it. I did not tell him, but I thanked God and Jesus and North Polian Elves for bringing him back to me.

"Who who who," he said softly in my ear. He tucked my arm in and held my hand, making two giant spoons on a couch made too small for reconciliation snuggles.

I tried to speak through my squashed cheeks. "You are one unfriendly Santa."

"You misbehaved. So I went and got snow."

I had misbehaved. I admit that freely now. I admit it now that it doesn't matter.

"I suppose we're even then."

"I'm sorry for what I said." I nodded forgiveness. "What do you say? Christmas in bed?"

It was all I wanted to do. And now that he was back in my realm I wanted the clock to tick so slowly we never once woke up and said, "It's tomorrow already?"

"Can we take a shower first? I'm still dirty from yesterday." If he stuck his nose any further down into my collar he would smell my sweat, his sweat, day-old lovers' quarrel, and his balls.

Pat got up off of me and held out his hand. "Let's go soap up your dirty parts."

I left a trail of clothing on our path to the bathroom, watching him smile with each piece left behind. He shut the door behind us and cranked the water on so that steam billowed over the curtain rod while he undressed. I leaned against the sink watching him. He blushed, which I found endearing. It dawned on me that we both were naked and we both were vulnerable, and we both felt something equally dreadful and magnificent when another person admired the parts of our bodies that we usually camouflage with strategically colored fabrics. Underneath we were all the same even though we are all so beautifully unique.

We showered a decadent thirty minutes, partly because it was Christmas, partly because it was fun, partly because it was the last time we would feel that way. It was everything a shower with another person is supposed to be. Slippery and sudsy, no crevice left unturned. Giggly, like we were getting away with something our parents would say we were too young for. Tender, for instance the reciprocal shoulder massages, washing each other's hair. It felt like time stopped for us, and all around us the hot mist protected us like a force field, like outside that room the world was hustling by, people were moving too quickly, logging none of the day in their memories, just going about their interpersonal connections like they were a chore to check off the list, like outside the bathroom life was simply being alive, no time to actually live. Behind the shower curtain we looked into each other's eyes and saw all the way down each other's throats, whirled around our bellies like hummingbirds, and then back up so that every word out of our mouths tip-toed the tightrope between joy and tears.

We also got real and talked about his deployment. We discussed what time he would be leaving the next day, how long he would be away, what little he could tell me about his exact location, "think Biblical," he said, and how serious the danger might be there. Gone were my panicked accusations, the doubts I had no right to or were insignificant on the scale of his life to come. It didn't matter that this whole relationship was a manifestation of everything that was wrong with us. It only mattered that he would be gone the next day, and so this day together mattered more than any day I'd lived up until then.

We talked about it all very sensibly, like these were the facts of our lives and I only needed to know for scheduling purposes, to know what time to wake up in the morning. The tail end of that sentence, *to know what time to wake up in the morning...to say goodbye forever*, was never uttered, implied, or hinted toward. It didn't even float around us in the mist. It went right down the drain with the shampoo. goodbye

I asked him why he was so normal. Why wasn't he shell shocked? Why didn't he wake up in the middle of the night with the sweats? Why wasn't he a PTSD cliché? How come when I walked around with the flashlight the night the power was out, he didn't scream "VC!" and strangle me with an electrical cord.

"Well, first of all because this isn't 1968," he joked. Always joking.

I traced his shoulder with my fingers, letting the water hit my back for this shift. We traded off every couple of minutes if we weren't clamped close enough that the water hit us both anyway. "You know what I mean." He stared over my head at nothing. "No freak outs? I know you've seen some shit over there."

He shrugged. "I guess I haven't really." But he swallowed, and we are far enough in this book to know what the swallow means by now.

I accepted it, didn't push him, didn't need to. He felt me examining him, felt exposed, and so he pulled me close to him. We revealed a lot in those few days, availed ourselves to each other's curiosity with an unnamed trust. But some stuff was off limits. What I could have done was scrape my insides for every insecurity I was afraid to admit aloud, give him the invitation to be so free with me, too. But I didn't. I left them inside me so he could, too. We kept those things for ourselves.

We stood there in a hug, and despite nothing fitting where it was supposed to and the weight of his arms crushing my lungs, I stayed as long as he would let me. And he did, too.

But my water heater was manufactured sometime around the Pleistocene era, so gradually our sexy shower turned into a tepid yawner. That was our cue.

He got out and toweled me off, paying a little extra attention to my boobs. "These things are soaking wet!" I brushed my hair, and he sat on the edge of the tub watching as though he'd never seen how we do that, us women folk. I lubed us both up with moisturizer, which he claimed to hate, "I feel like a ham," but he smiled as though he got off on the attention. We were spotless, flushed in the cheeks, our smiles radiating off our faces like our back teeth were begging to be noticed already. It was the most relaxed I'd ever felt in my life. I didn't want to open that door.

But then the second intruder happened, and it blew every fucking thing.

I knew something was amiss when over Pat's shoulder through the frosted glass of the bathroom window, a shadow passed like a dart. It seemed off, a man sized figure in the snowy field just outside. A wiser person might have reacted quicker so as to better improve our chances of saving everybody's lives. But I was drunk on romance and entranced by the perceived safety of this mist cloud force field I mentioned a few paragraphs back.

There was a clamor, the sound of a little kid learning to walk, if that kid was wearing hiking boots and reeked of morning brewskies. I could smell it through the bathroom door. Beer, whiskey, filth. And then it all happened in a flash.

I only knew what was happening by the look on Pat's face. His forehead and cheeks went from at-ease-soldier to atten-hut in one blink, and his eyes lit up like cannon fire. I heard the door knob turn, old houses have squeaky everything. Pat jumped from the edge of the tub and threw me out of the way. I flew against the tile and felt instant bruises form on the ribs that smacked against everything pointy sticking out from the shower wall.

Before I could land the door flung open and Pat was in animal mode. Everything primal and instinctive shot up and out from his gut to his fists. From behind I saw him battle Dale Lovejoy, naked, wet hair, his shoulder muscles lighting up here and there in a sequence like a spaceship control board. It was an even fight. Pat was a few inches shorter, but younger and clearly more physically fit. Dale was a naturally bigger guy, all mass and intimidation he'd been burdened with since childhood. And both had a fire in them they kept stoked but only let rage in times like these.

I worried and wondered how I could step in. They fought in the doorway and there was no way to get passed them to find a phone and dial anything, or a knife and stab something, or clothes and dress someone. Besides, anyone who has seen a serious fist fight where both participants intend serious harm knows things move pretty rapidly, and the frenzy of it all is disturbing to witness. It ain't like in the movies, when one guy swings, and then they exchange snappy one-liners, "Are we fighting or are we ballroom dancin'?," and then the other guy gets to throw a punch. No, in real life limbs fly too quickly to know whose are whose, and the sound of fists meeting bone surges through you like it's your very own brain being rattled inside your skull. It's grunts and growls, and blood and sweat rush, and there is no control, and thus a very fine line between a broken nose and manslaughter. In short it is terrifying to wait and see how far it goes.

Scarier still were the two glimpses I caught of Dale's face between blows. We locked eyes between Pat's swinging shoulders, just for a moment, and I realized he was there for me. I cowered naked in the tub, indifferent to that detail at the time, caring most about the fact that if Pat failed to subdue him, I was next. I smelled his drunken fury and saw a demon stare back at me, and I shook. I got my traction in case the time came to fight for my life.

But this was unnecessary for Pat was no less incensed and therefore Dale wasn't going to get a foot closer to me. With one good knock to the temple, Dale went down to a knee and I watched as his eyes rolled back in his head. I'd never seen a person faint before much less be knocked out. It creeped me out, still does. It haunts me that for a few seconds Dale's brain was smacked so haywire his spirit jumped out of his body, leaving behind a blank face, a beating heart, and drooped shoulders.

This should have been a signal to stop, that Pat had won the fight and he could run around the house with his fists over his head like a championship belt was at stake. But he didn't stop. He swung at Dale's head again and again, blood spray flying from his mouth, leaving impromptu Pollock paintings on my bathroom walls.

I screamed for him to stop, but even to me my voice sounded like it was coming through a drive-thru speaker. He swung and I yelled until finally I got out of the tub and grabbed his bicep from behind, hoping to break the spell. But in a reflex he thrust me off of him so that I propelled back into the tub again, this time smacking my head on the tile and watching the world wiggle in and out of my field of vision. Things went blurry, then multiplied, then went black, then became clear again.

Even being able to see and being aware of where I was, what year it was, who the president was and how many fingers I was holding up, my legs hadn't caught up to my brain yet. By then Pat had stopped punching Dale's body and hovered over him from his knees. Dale was in a heap on the ground and wasn't moving, and I still sometimes come out of the shower and see a ghost version of this exact scene when Pat swayed in a daze, like he was processing what his body had just done, calculating the consequences, trying to figure out where his brain went during the melee.

"Pat?" I squeaked, which seemed to snap him back to. He turned and rocketed to my side, covering me with a towel and bringing me into his arms. I cringed, everything ached, and the adrenaline came, reducing me to uncontrollable tremors. His eye was swelling quickly and his flesh was covered in big red blotches. "What happened?" I asked from inside Pat's chest.

He didn't answer. It was too macabre to explain to a person like me, or for him to make his mouth say. He huddled with me for what seemed too long, because breaking from that embrace meant calling the police and dealing with the fracas legally.

"He's dead, isn't he?"

"Decommissioned," Pat answered softly.

"You have to get out of here."

He pushed me out and away so he could see my face. "What?"

"You have to go. You will be arrested."

"So what? It's self defense."

"They won't even question me since I'm a girl."

"Marin. You're talking crazy."

But I felt clear as a bell in this decision. He was the one who had stepped out of his body just a few moments prior. If a police officer asked him what had just happened, I doubted he'd even be able to answer the question. And then he would be demonized, an Army statistic, and it would be a no brainer to arrest the wild man with the combat history and combat insanity, and there would be a subsequent insanity plea. Nothing would humiliate him more.

Honestly though, I couldn't argue against that. It was true that he'd gone mad in a flash, however one could justify if it they tried hard enough. But the fact is he killed Dale Lovejoy, no matter what terminology Pat was comfortable with, and someone was going to have to answer for it. "I will say I hit him with the hand soap dispenser until he was down."

"Are you fucking nuts?"

"I'll say everything happened as it did. I'll just take you out of the story." He put his hand over my mouth, but I smacked it away. "You will be arrested, Pat. You won't ship out. You will be discharged for this. It's possible a jury will look at this as excessive. There's no way they're going to send me to jail if I'm a hundred pounds lighter than him, and there's record of me in a previous police report involving him attacking a woman. I know what I'm talking about here. I will be fine."

"You watch too much TV. You could go to jail, too."

I took his hand and opened it. "You need to hit me a few times." He yanked his hand away from me and shook his head. I grabbed his face and forced him to hear me. "If you don't hit me, I'll just do it myself with something worse than your hand. Trust me on this one."

Pat sat back on his knees and put his head down. He knew this was the only way, but needed a second to weigh the morality of it all, to determine if he was breaking any personal code and if this was something he could live with.

"Do it," I ordered him.

"Shut your eyes," he told me.

"No. I need to see it coming." I welled up, knowing it was going to hurt and that neither of us wanted any more violence that day.

Then, before I could ready myself, he mercifully planted one on me so hard and suddenly I flew from his grasp and hit my face on the tub faucet. My cheek opened up and blood gushed out before I could even turn back to face him. "That should do it," I said, choking on shock.

"Fuck, fuck, fuck," Pat agonized, holding my jaw gently to look at me. But I wouldn't let him focus on that. I took his hands, still bloody with Dale's face all over them, and rubbed them in and out of my fingers, transferring the evidence onto me. "Jesus Christ, we can't do this."

"It's done. Get dressed and go. The longer we wait, the less believable this is."

"What will you tell the police?"

"Pat, go." It wouldn't be a problem. One person's account is a lot easier to believe and keep straight than two. Any cop would sniff out Pat's Army rage instantly, and Dale would go from being a murderous wife beater to a wrong-place-wrong-time Christmas casualty the local news would salivate over. Pat needed to be gone so I could clean this incident up, and get to marketing myself as a heroic victim so the police would stamp CASE SOLVED on the file and move onto the next, assuming they had a stamp for that.

I ask myself all the time why I would do such a thing. I honestly don't know how I decided so quickly to risk so much. But it wasn't optional in those few seconds of strategizing. In the tub, in the instant it was clear Dale was dead, the plan flew from my Ninja Control Center out of my mouth like nuclear fission, like I couldn't catch it if I tried. It wasn't impulse, it was the only possible solution, and so all my muscles, bones, and organs got on board right away. There's no other explanation.

I didn't let him wash his hands or face, the blood now coagulated to a thick gel in his razor stubble. I concentrated on getting every possible clue he'd been there and had him take it with him. There could be no tie to me whatsoever. He dressed in a tear and I looked at the clock, urging him to hurry.

"Fuck, Marin. Don't rush me." He slid on his snow boots, patted his pocket for his wallet, and then looked pained that he was ready to go, had everything on his person that he came with and goodbye was upon us. I was still in a towel, would remain that way for authenticity's sake. We stood in the hallway. Dale rested in a bloody pile a couple feet away. Pat jingled his keys and stared at me. His eyes were big, he bit his lip. I could see he was being pushed and pulled by his conscience, an otherwise virtuous attribute doing him no good here. He didn't know what to say.

"Be safe," I said.

This was it. No Christmas sex. No kisses in my doorway, resigned and at peace with our expired love affair. No watching from the kitchen window as his truck drove away and I allowed a bittersweet tear to make its way to my lips, as I'd imagined it would. Our goodbye was his guilt and my shaking hands, and the blood that was crusting down in my fingernail beds. My cheek was beginning to throb. Awareness was on its way.

"Your face," he said in a whisper.

"You can't contact me, Pat." He heard me swallow back panic. He threw his chin up and looked at the ceiling, thwarting the tears of his own that were coming. He shook his head. I nodded, cancelling him out. "It has to be that way."

"I'll be home next year."

The crying hurt my open gash, but I steeled myself and held up my hand. "Pat." I tried to ease him with my eyes, calm his boyish utility, like there needed to be a fix, like he needed to see some resolution, like he needed me at all. I breathed in deep and squared my shoulders. "This was the original plan, remember?

Nothing has changed." But of course everything had changed. This was a permanent link to me. A morbid tale sprung from what would have been a story about a winter fling that faded little by little over the years. What would have been "I wonder whatever happened to that Marin girl…" was now a battle bond he normally reserved for Army buddies who knew what he knew about war. Everything changed and there was no way to pretend all was how we had planned. But bold faced lie or not, I wanted him to believe I was secure in my decision, and I was prepared for what I would face after he left. "Now leave so I can call the police."

We kissed one last time, about a foot from where we did the first time, when I thought my heart was going to grow lungs and sing. The kiss was romantic and tragic and I remember all of it, how long it took, which way our heads tilted, the exact amount of pressure of his face on mine. I absorbed it because I knew I had to. Days would pass and I would wonder if I could trust my memory.

And then he was gone. I didn't see him out, just took one last pass through the house to make sure it was clear I was alone all day, and then dialed the police.

When they arrived there was no trouble convincing them I was distraught. I was distraught after all. In a week's time my life had changed in a way I could never tell another living soul, and

had no plans to, with or without the dead body in my bathroom.
My original vision was to love Pat for his perfection, however
imaginary, knowing full well a month longer with him and I would
have noted his flaws and kept them like a tally against all his good
qualities, which would seem less and less like good qualities and
more annoying quirks, so that in the end it would all add up to a
failing grade. In a week he was one big honeymoon, and he was
my momentary freedom. I chose to hang onto that as a reality.
Though I never could have had that experience without having
eventually said goodbye, it was still the best I'd ever felt in my
life.

In the living room I sat in my bath towel, sobbing. The
house quickly swarmed with police. Apparently a dead body
warrants an infestation. A choreographed team comes in and
examines every doorway, even ones I hadn't used in days, retraces
the victim's steps ten times over, then mine, swabbing everything
possible, talking into their walkies and cell phones, photographing
everything, including my hands, face, feet, and the faucet I'd gone
cheek first into. A female police officer in sweet tones asked if she
could take me to a private room to photograph the rest of my body,
which ached and I knew would give her some great shots. I cried
and nodded yes.

In the guest bedroom I took down my towel and covered my swimsuit areas with my hands. I caught in a full length mirror huge welts down my rib cage, right next to my aging bruises. There was an open wound on my spine, I guessed from the faucet the first time I collided with it. "Some of these bruises look older," she remarked calmly.

My eyes went dark and I laughed. "Those are from sex." Her eyebrows arched as she kept snapping the camera. "Unrelated."

She smiled. "You're doing fine. Just a few more."

I gave my statement over and over again, being sure not to include too much more detail every time. I told them my head hurt from one of Dale's first punches, so they sifted through my hair to look closer at it. I cringed as they touched it, hoped there were no tile fragments in it to blow my story. Apparently it had developed into a nasty lump and they winced at the sight of it.

They asked me if I had been raped, again and again, cop after cop. I shook my head vigorously, which made my brain feel loose and soupy. They asked why I thought he came to hurt me in the first place. I said I assumed it was retribution for my testimony. No one debated this, as I expected. They showed great concern for what they were sure was a concussion and suggested I get to a hospital. I resisted at first, but the nausea was moving toward unbearable, so I complied.

The lady cop stayed with me as I dressed. She could sense my unsteadiness, emotionally and physically. Getting my pants on had never been harder. At my drunkest I'd never had so much trouble finding the leg hole. Nothing seemed to fit how it was supposed to, how I remembered it to. I forgot to put on underwear or a bra, just sleepwalked into an argyle sweater and khaki trousers, which the cop had to adjust at the hem like a mother would her child's. "Here we go," she soothed, and we made our way out to the ambulance. The cop draped a coat over my shoulders as we walked slowly, a parade of wretched vulgarity for all my neighbors to gawk at, staring at me like strangers in their bathrobes and holiday themed attire. I stared back, and they looked away.

Dale's truck was parked at a forty five degree angle on the Lovejoys' snow covered lawn. It appeared while Pat and I showered and cooed that ol' drunk Dale came back to the scene, hoping to crash Nancy and Michael's Christmas, boldly claiming his marital and parental rights, not to mention his dog. I knew from a casual encounter with Nancy just a couple days before that she was spending the holiday out of state, with her family, to be as far away from him as possible, and create new traditions. I learned much later Dale had been out on bail a week and by then had been contacting her relentlessly, so perhaps she was running.

It hit me someone was in pursuit of Nancy now to tell her I'd killed her husband. I had no idea how she might take that. Not good, I supposed. Beaten wives can be complete whackos regarding their abusers, particularly when they are brutally killed on Jesus' birthday.

Stepping into the ambulance I realized this was the same ponytailed paramedic who treated Nancy not too long ago, in my living room, in her bra, with her son looking on. Evidently my neighborhood was on his beat. "Come here often?" I asked him grimly.

He eased me in and laid me down on a stretcher for a quick once over. He shot a pen light into my right eye. "This is when you say 'You should see the other guy.'"

I smiled. "You *should* see the other guy," but then it dawned on us both what poor taste this cliché was when the other guy was presently being zipped into a body bag. Simultaneously our faces fell.

The paramedic shut the back door to keep the heat in. As the light muted around us I saw Dale's DOGNUTS license plate disappear behind the doors. "Let's see what this guy did to you," the Ponytail said, and turned my head delicately away from him.

I shut my eyes and trusted him with his work. I would have to open them back up soon enough.

XI.

The days following Pat's departure from America and Dale's from Earth, I did what anybody does after Christmas. I scrubbed blood and hair off my walls, carpet, and bathroom tile. I squirted antibacterial spray onto my face stitches, iced the back of my head, stretched the tightness out of and the oxygen into my ribs and spine. The holidays can be a bitch for us all.

Jane returned from her travels abroad and had stories for me she knew I would just die over. Just *die*, she claimed. I doubted so. She called and said she was coming over with souvenirs and photos and wasn't taking no for an answer. I conveyed interest.

When I answered the door though, it appeared *she* would just die. Immediately she gasped at my black and blue face and the crust of no discernable color forming around my stitches, and covered her mouth with her hand.

"I know, I know. Come in," I tugged at her arm.

"What the fuck happened?" She dropped her purse and came very close so that her nose nearly touched mine. "That's so disgusting." She reached out and almost touched my face, but decided against it.

I laughed convincingly. "It's fine. I was mugged."

"Mugged? Who gets mugged anymore?"

"Plenty of people."

"Really?"

"It's Christmas. People are desperate."

"Are you okay?"

I grinned, "Of course. Shut up. Sit down. You're home!" She followed me to the couch, stunned. Was this how I looked at Nancy? If so, apologies were in order. First for my reaction to her wounds, second for killing her son's father. "How was Rio?"

"Did he rape you?"

"God, why does everyone ask me that? No. He hit me with his gun and ran away. It's not a big deal." I'd stolen that from every crime drama I'd ever watched on TV. "I cancelled my credit cards. It's fine."

"Did you call the police?"

"Of course," I replied impatiently.

"Did they catch him?" She reached out and touched my knee, not to comfort me, but to have something to lean against while she got eyeball to eyeball with my flesh wound.

"Not yet. But they will." I grabbed her hands and forced her attention. "I'm fine. It will heal. I'm not worried about it. I'm just happy to see you." I hid behind my eyes, even with her. Even with the one who would accept it all, since she, cloaked in her own fresh stitches and mystery on occasion over the years I'd known her, likely understood what can happen when the fairy tale veers off course. Didn't matter though. I kept it all inside.

Jane sighed and accepted it. "What an adventure, huh?" I nodded. "Story for the grandkids." I smiled. "So no rape?"

"No rape."

"Not even fondling?"

"I would welcome some fondling right about now. It's been a while. I'm not picky. Criminals are welcome. Fondle away!"

She found that hilarious and went into a story about some heavy petting she'd experienced on a Brazilian bus ride a week before flying home. The man spoke no English other than American brand names, and she spoke no Portuguese other than foods and beverages, and so they communicated with their hands and facial expressions, and eventually their tongues. She growled desperately, "I love him!" The sort of tongue one takes home to Mama, I suppose.

"What his name?"

"I don't know!" She laughed. "I'll never see him again. But I don't care. It was so beautiful. We connected."

"On a bus?" She nodded. "A moving bus?"

She didn't bother with my subtle judgment. "It was such a rush. I know we'll remember each other forever. Like, he's thousands of miles away, but we share this," and she flattened a palm against her heart. From a make-out session on a bus, which I could safely surmise was hurtling down a dirt road at the time, and perhaps this is an insensitive generalization, but I imagine there to be live chickens running up and down the aisle. "And even when we're old, we'll both remember that. It's ours."

I agreed. I actually understood what she meant for once. "Like you're holding a tin can, and he's holding a tin can, and there's a string connecting them."

"Yes! Oh!" Jane groaned beautiful anguish. "So romantic. I'm going to send him signals forever and ever." She was talking like a boy-crazed thirteen year old, the type of thirteen year old who gave handies in the back of public buses. Foreign ones.

Forever and ever.

I knew that feeling. I imagined what Pat was doing every second since he'd left. I wondered at what point I would be off his mind, wondered if I would be able to sense it and feel pain knowing he had never left mine. I wondered at what point he would go a day without remorse and the alarming reality that he killed someone with only his hands once. I wondered if he sat in the mess hall with his comrades, all of them with their own stories from leave, and he worried how I was, whether I was in jail, whether I had undergone any real physical harm that he didn't know about without the benefit of x-rays and professional medical attention.

I transmitted to him with every electrical pulse of my being the words, "I'm okay," over and over again while doing simple tasks. Washing the dishes, driving the car, standing in the shower where it all went down. I touched the tile like he was in there somewhere and whispered, "I'm okay," softly aloud, but with all the force my heart and brain could muster so that they shot through space from my tin can to his tin can in his dusty outpost in the middle east, so that if it lost momentum along the way, perhaps faced some headwinds or turbulence, at least a faint comfort would reach him. I cried every day, all day, not because I missed him or because I was horrified by what we shared. I cried because I know a man like him carries all of that too heavy inside of him. He would never be able to share the experience with anyone else, never be able to drop his burden on anyone else, and no matter how his life progressed and what he achieved, that forlorn look around his eyes and across the lines in his forehead were permanent. The week, the sex, Dale's tragic end. It was ours, forever and ever.

It's funny. When you're recovering from something like this, you tell yourself the future is near. It's *here* even. Every second passing in pain is a second that's already passed. It's off your shoulders, so just be patient. A survivor says to herself that there are blue skies coming, just wait. Just keep waiting. This is how we get through life's defeats, whether it be a death in the family, or unrequited love, or professional failure. Wait and be patient. All will be well.

We busy ourselves as though time will pass quicker that way, like distraction is the same as healing, when really all it does is replace what little room we have in our day for pain with trivial duties. If I reorganize my closets and do my taxes months earlier than they are due, I won't feel this horrible suffocating loss that pulls my gut through my tailbone and chokes me as I try to sleep at night. But when you finish all your tasks and your life appears best represented by a neat stack of professionally folded sweaters ordered by color and season in perfect geometric precision, you free up that space in your brain, because there's nothing left to do, and the pain settles back in. You lay in your bed with your freshly spread sheets, and suddenly you realize that choking sensation is real, and it's Dale's tennis racquet sized hand around your throat, and as you kick your feet to free yourself, you realize it isn't Dale, it's Pat choking you, and all the terror comes back, and then you wake up sweating like a filthy pig and those freshly spread sheets are tomorrow's new chore.

A month after Pat left I went to work at one point and looked over my cubicle wall. I originally stood to yawn and stretch, get my blood flowing in the afternoon lull. I had spent those recent few days functioning more normally. My stitches were gone and I looked less science fiction and more Marin, and I'd begun smiling at strangers again. Life was falling into routine, and so a stretch from a desk chair would have been just that any other day.

This day at work though I saw across the sea of half-walls a girl I barely knew. We'd crossed paths at the coffee maker a thousand times. I knew her name but never addressed her by it in the off chance I had it wrong, because she would probably never correct me, we are all so overly polite, and then I would go months calling her Kristen when her name was actually Kirsten. This is a real paranoia of mine, so instead it was, "Good morning," whether or not it was, an occasional "did you have a nice weekend?" but for the most part always stood out of her reach. My "how are yous" were the sort one asks when they don't really want to know the answer, particularly since an accurate answer likely involves a family feud, maybe some nagging flatulence, mother issues, an overwhelming sense of purposelessness, a quiet and suffocating suburban depression. I use "how are you" as a silence filler, and I always sensed this girl did, too. She was friendly but didn't exactly throw confetti at me when I walked in the room.

Around us the office buzzed and phones rang, but she sat at her desk, motionless. She was leaning back in her chair with her forehead in her hand. I thought it might be a moment of frustration, or the same afternoon coma we all suffered, but she stayed there for far too long, and when she broke from it she held her hand to her lips, staring into the gray fabric of her cubicle wall. She sat perfectly still, processing internally. I wondered what it might be, this distress paralyzing her. No one had been gossiping about her that day, so whatever it was it was for her to feel alone.

Later I saw her in the bathroom and we washed our hands in adjacent sinks. She seemed fine. I gave her a half ass smile, friendly but meaningless, she gave the same back to me and left. It was all very clean. No emotion. No actual exchange occurred. It was two warm bodies orbiting in opposite gravitational fields. At her core she boiled, but on the surface she was just a girl, verging on anonymous, washing her hands, taking a break from the grind.

From there I deliberated on everyone. The happiest people I left alone, because they were the most obvious ticking time bombs of all. The negative nellies who brought the room down with their interminable bereavement weren't of any interest either, because people who wear their hearts on their sleeves most likely just weren't hugged enough as children.

It's the in-betweens I obsess over now. They are more common than I would have figured, now that I'm looking for them. There is a quiet calm that unnerves me. The happy people and the sad people will shout their pain from the closest mountaintop, or flat surface for that matter. But those in the middle, they will endure privately for a lifetime.

I spent that month writing everything I could down. January is the deepest pit of winter, and despite it being a new year and all that represents, in actuality everything is dead or asleep. I knew spring would come soon and I would forget much of this. Optimism would bring with it God's blessing to move on. The season would change and He would say from whatever cloud He was on that it was symbolic of our own personal renewal, and I should feel free to let Pat go. Even though the wind whipped a deep freeze into the world around me, rolling over the field behind my house in tufts of snow like angel wings, I still felt spring coming and feared what blew in with it.

So I wrote it all down. Jokes he told, the things I'd confessed to him, and him to me, the meals we ate, the reasons he was beautiful and special, his approximate height, his facial features and the stories of his high school football battle wounds, even some of the milder adult battle wounds he let me be privy to, and no one else. I put it all in a leather journal, all of this priceless information I couldn't buy if I tried. The only thing I didn't put in there, because I didn't know it, was his last name. All that time, unintentionally or intentionally, I wasn't sure which, I had never asked, and he never volunteered it.

How strange that if I wanted to track him down and called up the Army in Afghanistan and said, "Yes, I'd like to speak with Pat?" and they said, "Pat who?" and I said, "You know, he's about 6'1", couple hundred pounds, has an eagle tattoo and a roman nose, loves grilled cheese sandwiches," they would laugh and wonder which of their soldiers had knocked me up in a one night stand. How odd, because it would appear I was asking for a stranger, when it was possible I knew him better than anyone else. I couldn't exactly say, "You know, Pat. The one who is harboring anger toward his dad for leaving him in military school so soon after his mother's passing, and who now keeps a withered letter she wrote on her death bed in his wallet? That Pat. His last name escapes me."

We assign so much identity to people based on their basic stats, what's on their driver's licenses and W-2s. But really, none of us knows each other at all. And that's the way we like it.

XII.

After all that time I still had a muted shadow of Dale's
blood in my house, no matter which super toxic cleaner I bought
from late night infommercials. I put it to mind that I would retile,
paint the walls, lay down some new carpet. It would be nice to
spruce things up anyway, whether or not someone had
hemorrhaged there once.

Until then though I stood atop it like the truth never
happened. I suppose if I was wracked with guilt perhaps I could
have moved out or something. But I didn't so much as throw a bath
rug over the stain. I am a peace loving person and like to believe
someone victimized Dale once in his younger days, and it was for
this reason he lacked any humanity with the one person in his life
he should have trusted the most. I couldn't imagine the flurry of
hell he lived through every day, like his very own untangled
necklace, and he couldn't figure out how to sort through it. There
was probably a child inside him screaming for mercy, begging to
love someone and be loved, but the body around him wouldn't

allow for love. The beast holding Dale captive wanted to destroy, and as much as I would love to persecute him I am aware he was a product of his sick past, and therefore was sick himself.

Then my empathic self jumps forward to the day Nancy couldn't form words with her mutilated mouth, and her son spaced out on my couch, as the Ponytail determined if she'd have trouble eating for the rest of her life. This is the scene I think of most, not Dale's tortured youth. I am surprised now, considering the look in his eye while I trembled in the bathtub, that he didn't kill Nancy when he could. I am convinced if given the chance that Christmas morning, he may have, and possibly Michael, too.

I don't tell myself these things so I can live with what Pat did, which is to commit a crime. In fact I am haunted by Dale's ghost. I don't mean to say that I worry he judges me when I pick my nose. I don't worry that he watches me while I shower, waiting to flush the toilet until right when I get in. I don't worry that he will possess me and my head will spin, and I will levitate and barf all over a priest one day. These things don't remotely concern me. I pick my nose freely, and I pick often. This isn't the form his entity takes. Rather he lives on in the loss I feel in the quiet hours. If I sleep soundly, I dream of Pat. I dream of cross-country skiing. I dream of Lambeau nachos. I dream of Pat's white undershirts.

I am aware of course that Pat was a danger to the world to be capable of doing what he did. It is a happy accident that the one person in the world he snapped and beat the spirit out of just happened to be on a murderous rampage himself. Everybody won in this scenario, however another time may have come for Pat, a time I would never know about, when he flipped on a grocery store bagger, or a guy who cut him off in traffic, or an innocent civilian crossed paths with him on the wrong day on the job in Afghanistan. It's possible that having killed Dale made it easier for him to do it again, or that he could kill Dale so coldly because previous incidents he never told me about were a stepping stone to this. It is also possible the fear of doing it again would compel him to seek professional help. More likely though it strengthened his propensity for mechanical violence.

By keeping him out of jail, I see my culpability in someone else being harmed by Pat. I wish I could reconcile this using my relief that Dale is off the planet and in God's prison, and that in actuality Pat saved Nancy and Michael's life. I cannot though. And so when I saw Dale's blood stains in the waning days of winter, I prayed deep into my clasped hands that a force saved Pat from himself and spared any more victims by his military issued temper, deserving or otherwise. I said, "Remember that time I went to Mass and was mesmerized by what you've built?" I said this to Him like we're bros now. I tried to get him on my side so I could persevere and live with this teeter-totter position I had put myself in.

I didn't see Nancy for quite some time. Not once, in fact, since Pat killed her husband. She was so crippled by the negativity emanating from our city block that even when the *For Sale* sign went up in her yard, and carbon copy realtors in identical feathered hair and business separates flowed in and out of her house like an ant trail, she never once reared her head.

I knew for a fact she was selling too low. I'd bought my house for $10,000 above her asking price, and she had 500 more square feet and a finished basement. Clearly Nancy wanted to unload that thing and all its contents to anyone willing. The horror stained couch and wrath wreaked four-poster bed were included, a nice little bonus to the quickest bidder. The poltergeist was complimentary.

It only took a couple of weeks and the *SOLD* placard was positioned atop her yard sign. I was comforted by this. I feared what sort of sadist was moving in her place, worried it would be someone who would want to take down the fence between us and have joint Fourth of July barbeques. I would take a house full of reclusive meth cooks over suburban congeniality. But I was happy to see Nancy moving on. Happy for us both, I suppose.

One late night I heard a knock at the door. I knew it was her. No one else ever knocked but Pat, and I'd given up on the daydream of that happening again long before. I'd let go of the vision of me opening the door, looking accidentally ravishing of course, and having him sweep me up into his arms and putting his dress uniform hat on my head while a seventies era love song swelled to a crescendo in the background. By then I'd settled on it being a fantasy instead of an actual possibility, and I'd come to a point it being only a fantasy did not choke me up. Took me a while, but I got there.

So Nancy knocked, and I hesitated as I always did. I figured though that this would be the last time I ever spoke with her, so I should just suck it up and answer it.

I opened the door and she stood there with Honorico, the four legged lint catcher, who looked skinny and weird. Dirty maybe. They both did in fact. It seemed showers and food were beyond what her dance card could accommodate for the time being, what with a funeral to attend and her entire life in upheaval. Her wrists seemed to wilt on the brittle old bones I called the rest of her body. I was unsettled by it.

"Nancy," I smiled, greeting her. Her shoulders were high on her frame, like she was nervous, holding her breath. She froze a moment. The gravity of her visit hit me, and I realized how hard it must have been for her to come to my door. I didn't know whether she was angry or embarrassed, but I knew in order for her to know I meant no harm to her, she had to be welcome in my home. I stepped aside to let her through. "There's a chill out there. Come inside."

She entered with caution with raggedy old Honorico, like he'd gone crotchety over the winter. She stood in the middle of the living room. I wondered what her opener would be. *So. You killed my husband. What was that like? And will you be planting those geraniums again this year?* I kind of hoped she would just get to it. I'd seen her mangled face on my doorstep just a few months prior. Pardon the pun, but tear off the bandage, lady. Let's say the unsaid. You'd think we'd be passed small talk by then. We'd certainly broken the ice. We should have nicknames and secret handshakes after all we'd been through. She could call me Fists of Fury and I could call her Face of Fury and we could go out for bourbons together. But no, she asked how I was.

Living the fucking dream, Nance. "I'm well. You?"

She nodded too heartily to be real. "We sold the house," she smiled with no teeth.

I put my hands in my pockets. "I saw that. Congrats." She had to have been rattled standing there. She was fifteen feet from her husband's stain, but never once looked in that direction. I didn't know what to do or say. "I'm going to sit if that's okay." I walked gingerly to the couch, avoiding any sudden movements. Still wasn't sure if she was there for revenge.

Nancy followed. Honorico wiggled down under the coffee table onto his belly, one of my feet caught underneath so I could feel his heartbeat through my sock.

"I came to apologize," she started.

I shook my head and gave her a conciliatory knee-tap. "Nancy, no."

"I didn't know he would come after you."

"Exactly. There's no way any of us could have known." Except for all those threatening phone calls ahead of time. Probably could have warned me he might turn up in the neighborhood with an axe to grind.

"I thought if he couldn't find us he would just give up on me."

"You must be pretty irresistible then," I joked. She smiled and looked down at her feet.

"I'm just so sorry."

"Nancy you need to stop this. Did it ever occur to you that if you were home that day, he probably would have killed you? He could have killed Michael." Her shoulders slunk forward and she welled up, ashamed. "I know it's awful what happened, but it's better than if any of us was seriously hurt, or worse. Right?"

"I just wish you didn't have to go through what you did."

"It's just a scratch," I placated her, realizing if we were ever in a bar strangers would think we work together at the local battery acid plant.

"No, not just that."

"My concussion? I was fine the next day." I tapped my head. There's still a notch there to this day, but don't tell her that.

"No, I mean…when he died."

Oh. That.

We talked a while longer, about where Nancy and Michael had been staying and the therapist she'd been seeing. She recommended I pay him a visit, said she called him Dr. Feelgood, a play on words she thought she made up and therefore said with pride. "If anyone should be seeing a doctor it's someone in your shoes." My shoes. My *homicidal* shoes, she left out. I suppose in her eyes if anyone was going to need psychological help it was someone who'd struck a man to death with a soap pump in her very own home. It probably should have disturbed her how unaffected I was by this tragedy, and that the morning after Dale's body was scooped up and out, I made chocolate chip waffles and watched cartoons for a couple hours. I missed Pat, so I ate. That was about it.

"I could not agree more," all lip service. "I wouldn't mind checking it out once or twice." Blah, blah, blah. I doubt Nancy bought it.

I asked how Michael was faring. Sure, he was free from the sort of home life where it was uncertain they would get through a meal without his mother being degraded, but this was still a boy without a father. Nancy said he'd been doing great, was benefitting from his new school like it was a clean slate, a new life. He spent a month or so feeling uncomfortable in his grandma's house, but eventually settled into doing chores and building forts and a regular sleep schedule like a normal kid. "It's amazing, isn't it? Their resilience?" she asked, hoping to convince us both. She stared off with a look of regret.

"I have a theory, Nancy."

"What's that?"

"I think kids who go through what Michael did turn out the best in the end."

She huffed, rolled her eyes. "Only people who haven't been parents say that."

She had me there. It was easy for me to say this from my safe distance. I didn't have to watch him with crossed fingers all his life to see how he reacted to his first love dumping him, or see how aggressively he behaved after a little league defeat and draw too many conclusions from it. I didn't have that pressure. I didn't have to apologize for my son's behavior to a school principal, even for normal adolescent folly, as though I was apologizing in advance for all the hookers he would strangle one day. I did my best to boost her anyway. "It's true. He'll be tough. He'll be responsible and protective of his mom. And when other kids give up, he'll know what he's made of and work harder than the others."

She rubbed the back of her neck. "Or he'll turn out like his daddy."

I wasn't going to say it, but she was probably right. The pendulum could swing either way, goodness knows how that sort of thing is decided by the fates. If I knew the recipe, what he would need to do to turn out a city prosecutor instead of a defendant, I would have written it down and passed it her way, no charge. But it really was a crap shoot this early in his life.

We talked more and I could sense she was still very fragile, and not just because she was literally fragile, what with this new prepubescent bone mass she was dragging around. In a few months her life had been dismantled. People who didn't know her had to wait for the right time to ask what the hell happened to her face, gauge when the appropriate time was to bring it up, if to at all. She could see it in their eyes, and so she wore a lot of hats and sunglasses, was thankful it was still scarf season so as to justify such coverage. All of the people who did know her history never mentioned it, just let it hang in the air when they talked about frivolous shit, like what they should do differently with their hair this year, or the best place to go for an oil change. And maybe some of the people who didn't know the back story were perturbed with her appearance, like it was too much for their children to have to look at, and how dare she expose them to that. She couldn't walk through life with a secret pain even if she tried. I pitied her and hoped the years would pass and she would be a hero to herself one day.

Her future, Michael's, it was all anybody's guess. A shake of the 8-Ball read "Ask again later."

"I know it seems like it's going to be a long time before you feel good again. I really hope it won't be, because it's sad to know someone like you feels so isolated." She looked tired. Her eyes dropped and the corners of her mouth defaulted in the down position. Nancy was clinging to hope with the tips of her pinkies, but her grip was slipping. "And one day you'll meet someone special. And you'll know what all this was for."

Nancy scoffed, rubbed her nose and refused to meet my eye. "Right. There's a man out there looking for *this*." She waved her hand in front of her face, like even she didn't want to touch it.

"Of course there is." I hoped there was.

"I don't think I want to meet anyone."

"Sure, I understand. It'll be a while before you're ready."

She shook her head. "That's not what I meant." Nancy paused and looked around my living room. The big empty living room with impersonal art on the walls, like I'd moved into a model home. As she processed her thoughts, I could sense her analyzing me using that room alone. "I get sad when I meet good people." She laughed. "Isn't that awful?"

This was a new one. "You get sad?"

"You haven't noticed how rare good people are?" Of course I had. The nightly news had. Every person I'd ever encountered who said things like "there's just no courtesy anymore" had. My lack of friends and overabundance of acquaintances whose last names I never bothered to ask were all the meter I needed. "When you're young, you're friends with everybody. It doesn't matter if they're slime balls. You just want to be popular. But then you get older and realize you just want to know nice people. The problem is there aren't any left."

"I'm sorry. I'm still not following."

She took a breath. "I met someone nice in my support group. Margie. She's so smart. She's been through what I've been through. Worse. And I feel like she really wants to be my friend. But I have a hard time with it. It's hard to explain why."

"Be her friend, Nancy. It sounds like she needs someone like you as much she you need someone like her."

She got frustrated. She shook her head wildly enough some of her hair fell out of her newly graying bun. "No. You're not listening." So thin. The muscles in her neck stuck out like big old oak roots. How fitting, those old oaks have seen a lot in their time, too.

I slowed her down with my hands, pumping the metaphorical brakes. "Okay, go ahead."

A tear fell. "When I talk to her, I try to remember the last time I met someone like her. You know, anyone who gets me. And you know what? There's no one. I think it's been fifteen years since I came across someone I can trust, longer maybe. All that leads me to believe is that we're all alone. We're just," throwing her hands up in disgust, "alone." She slouched back in the couch so that her chin rested on her chest, like she was giving up on everything, including posture.

And by God, she was right.

This is what I was mourning once Pat left. Yes, I missed him so damn much. I wanted him back to love me and know and accept me. I wanted him to just write me a God damned fucking letter which read that he had no intentions initially of falling in love with me, but he did, and we will deal with that together. And if there could be no letter, I wanted to wait for him and go to our bar every night hoping he would return and lose control a second time with me, and compulsively smother me in kisses like a dog and his long lost owner, and I didn't care if I was the dog or the owner in the scenario, so long as it happened. I wanted to climb on him and demand his full attention as he told me everywhere he'd been and everything he'd done that he felt good about, and tell him about my mundane comings and goings without him and let him tell me they weren't so mundane and look at me like my ineffectual life was as important as his and as interesting to hear described. I wanted to have tons of sex with him and stare directly into his face so he would know I'd been waiting impatiently to mold into him and dig my fingernails into his skin like an animal in a tree hanging on for dear life.

Of course I missed every ounce of him. But I know now harder than the awareness that he wasn't coming back and would never knock on my door again was that it would be miles of time and space before any other person would penetrate my defenses again. There would be no one worthy. I couldn't rely on running into a G.I. every Christmas and pitch to him a week long sex fest. Though it certainly catalyzed whatever the fuck Pat and I were, loosened my belt buckle, the one on my pants and the imaginary one I kept above the zipper to my secret self, I was admitting to myself then that he was more than convenient and comfortably temporary. He was also a nice, solid person who told good jokes and found me beautiful and understood me down to the quarks of my soul. He translated me back to me. And it would be forever before I happened upon that again. It was reason to never even want for it.

On my couch, where I was supposed to be comforting *her*, efficiently so I could get on with the goodbyes and on with my life, we cried together.

XIII.

Spring is better than summer, and here is why.

Summer is over before it's begun. First it's hot and you're grateful to be wearing shorts and can't even remember socks, but every day that passes you say to yourself you can't believe it's such-and-such a date. Whereas autumn and winter move at about the rate of going backward in time, right up to that point in January where you're sure the planet has actually stopped spinning and is so cold it's frozen into place, conversely summer whizzes by in a frenetic whirlwind. It feels like time-lapse photography. It is so much good you can't hold all of it at once and feel its preciousness before it's ripped out of your hands.

Spring though is that point when Copernicus, howling from the grave, looks at his watch and inserts his big ol' wrench into the core of Earth and cranks us back up again. First it comes slow, that one day when you notice all the snow on your block has melted and the shiny asphalt bears no unseen danger. Then a couple of days later one leaf, a single leaf, waves hello from that tree out back, and you stare at it obsessively, think about taking its picture, this pioneer leaf taking a risk and seeing if it's safe for all the others to follow suit. A week later he brings back some of his friends, and a week after that the first blue sky charges through town, no clouds necessary, like the coolest guy you went to high school with, home from college, and he's got some serious muscle tone these days.

It is energizing to see it all come very slowly, a new something every day. If not a new life form creeping out of the ground, it's the new pair of flip flops, or the first pull of your neighbor's lawnmower, or the first smell of charcoal lighter fluid. The grocer phases out the bags of salt and gradually replaces the display with Styrofoam coolers, and you, the patron, smile to yourself watching the season arrive in the form of commercial goods. Just a little bit new every day, and you forget all about winter as though it never happened. Here it is, a ten pound baby named Spring, and the joy that it brings erases from your memory what it took to pass that thing out of your body.

It's all brand new. I love it. Who doesn't love brand new?

I know we're nearing the end of this story, and things are taking a more positive tone than third degree murder by reason of insanity, and you as the reader are counting how many pages are left. You are saying to yourself Pat has only got this last chapter to appear back in Marin's life, with a bouquet of romantic tidings and all sorts of sentimental crap. I will cut to the chase though. This is not a love story, and it is not a chick flick. It might be time to go get a gallon of ice cream and a big spoon, no bowl necessary, if this is disappointing to you. I should probably inform you in fact that the very hallmark of love is disappointment, decaying from the moment it is born, like everything and everyone, and not an endless flame. Even endless flames are fueled artificially with accelerants after all. Like you and me and everything else in this world, love is always one second closer to death. Come to think of it, in that case if you were looking for a love story, well, you got it.

The point is that this story has come along to spring, when all that came the year before has melted down into my field out back. Pat and Nancy and the love and injury that came with them were the coat I wore all winter. Anyone who lives with seasons knows that the second you hang up your big wool coat one last time, you leave behind everything that season felt like. Being trapped indoors for so long, crowded by a maddening reality, the second the windows open up and suck out all the winter, it's time to live a new life, even if you're fabricating it every day.

I decided Honorico was mine. I presented this as an option to Nancy, that he live with me until the dust settled and they could afford a yard again, but that would be some time yet as Nancy and Michael had just moved into an upper nine hundred square foot apartment with nothing for Honorico to do but waste away and sigh. Technically I offered up my home as though this was optional, but in my mind had already decided his fortune so that she could gasp "thank you!" and weep relief. It was only right.

I don't particularly like dogs. Honorico is never clean. Never. When I wash him in the tub he shakes off solid chunks of mud and general outdoor debris on the tile walls. Once I found a live snail in his coat. He shakes at least eight or nine times, so I've taken to bathing him in the nude and then hosing myself off afterward. This is especially creepy when Honorico faces the doorway, right where his former master was killed, lovingly pining for Dale. I don't want to call this any sort of atonement, but if there is any debt owed to Dale and the justice Pat took into his own hands, caring for Honorico in his twilight will just have to suffice. One day I will bury this tired old dog in the backyard a stone's throw from Dale's ghost, and I will love him, or treat him as though I do, every day until then, and I should remind you dogs are pretty disgusting creatures. Even after his bath and shakes, he feels and smells like dirt covered in mildew with the faint mask of shampoo scent fooling no one. And I think sometimes he eats his own poop.

But we spend a lot of time together, me and the dog. The new neighbors moved in on the tail end of winter, a young couple with a little baby I hear crying sometimes, but mostly just gets shuttled around in one of those clunky carriers in a pink blanket so fluffy I couldn't say for certain there's an actual baby in there. A week after they were settled Honorico and I came home from a walk. He had gained and then lost some weight, mostly because I failed to buy actual dog food for a month and just fed him whatever I was eating, which happened to be bacon cheeseburgers and bacon omelets and bacon by itself while the winter layers still allowed for a little extra girth.

By then though he was back to his teenaged weight, and so broke from his leash to greet our new neighbor. He scared the shit out of the mother, who clutched her purse close to her like that would save her from the infamous golden retriever jaws of death.

"Rico! Heel!" I called after him, as though I had ever given him a command, taught him a command, or even knew exactly what he was supposed to do when I said "heel." I always imagined that would mean he was supposed to bow, but then realized that command is called "bow." I know now it means Honorico is supposed to dig his nose in a woman's crotch and root around as though there was a rawhide hiding in her cervix, since this is exactly what he did. He certainly had a way.

I reached him and tugged his collar away. "I'm so sorry."

"No, its finnnnne," she sang, like it wasn't completely awkward and the subtext didn't read *Smelly Vagina*.

"Welcome to the neighborhood," I reached out my hand to her. We introduced ourselves, I feigned comfort. She mentioned her husband was a firefighter and only home two or three nights a week, that she hosted a book club every other month, and she recently decided to quit teaching third grade to stay home with her little girl. This all seems like your basic chit chat, but I used it to calculate the odds she would want to be my friend. Absent husband + social predisposition + inductee into the "whatever Oprah does, I do" club + virtual daily isolation = 96% probability she would at least call or "swing by" daily. I use quotations because she looked like the sort of person who would use "swing by" like it was a cavalier thing to show up on my doorstep when I was trying to eat my bacon on a Saturday morning, in my underpants, in peace.

She was presently wearing a pastel pink cardigan. This did not bode well for me.

After she was done giving me her qualifications, I gave her a little of my own personal résumé. "Well, first off I don't have a steady lover, but I do sometimes bring a swarthy gal home from the gym with me. We are lesbians," just to clarify, "so don't be alarmed if you see a muscular woman sunbathing topless in the field out back. To answer your question in advance, no, those aren't her real breasts... I'm not a big reader, sorry. How about music? Do you like metal? Death metal, I mean? What are your thoughts on the new *Afterbirth* album? I can't stop playing it, personally." She smiled, shook her head and closed her sweater tight around her little frame. "Hmm, well, let me know if you ever need a sitter."

She edged back an inch or so. I'm not sure she realized she was doing it. "Yes. You seem very," clearing her throat, "maternal." As she said this Honorico was behind me, hunched and panting, dropping a huge dump in the middle of my driveway. "Dog nuts make great parents," she cringed.

Dog nuts. Yep.

She excused herself and went inside, and I watched as the screen door shut quietly behind her. I wondered if the house gave off any vibes, if she vacuumed up fear along with the dust. My conscience ruins me these days, so I knocked on her door.

"Hi again," she begrudged as she came to the door, opting not to open it and ask me inside.

"I'm not a lesbian."

She paused. "Okay."

"It's fine to be one. But I'm not."

She crossed her arms, thinking maybe she'd moved onto the corner of Freakazoid Ave. and Acid Trip Rd. "Okay."

"And I enjoy books. I read them. All sorts. So I would like it if I could be invited to your book club sometime. If you're interested." *Like* may have been a strong word. I could probably have used *survive* instead.

She forced a smile. "I will do that." Her baby started to cry in the other room and her shoulders jumped to attention.

"I'll leave you to that," I said. I backed away realizing she needed a minute to process me, a month maybe. I waved and turned onto the walk back up to my own front door. Honorico wagged his tail and trotted along side me, happy to have a new place to sniff in the neighborhood. I heard the creak of her screen door open and turned back to see her standing there.

"What about the death metal? Was that true?"

"Yeah. Sorry."

She shrugged and accepted it.

It was spring. A season for trying new things, being new things. This was all a very big step for me. It felt good.

One day Cherie and I sat on the back step and watched Honorico explore the field. Her baby was getting ready to exit her uterus already, making room for her sanity, I hoped. It had been a tense last few weeks, she confided, between her and her husband, since even average sized babies feel oversized when they're elbowing major internal organs. She complained that every minute was a struggle not to laugh or cough for fear of pissing her pants, and she didn't mean delicate squirts that could be disguised with a lit candle or spritz of perfume. She meant a complete bladder evacuation, leaving behind evidence that resembled what my ceiling looked like after this last severe rain storm that my old roof gave way to. I'd never seen her short fuse in all the time I'd known her, and here she was, thinking of taking up third trimester smoking just to calm her nerves.

"What made you want to adopt a dog?" she asked, befuddled. Cherie knew me well.

"Lonely, I guess."

"Yeah, but... a dog? You?" She knew me a bit too well.

"He needed a home." Neither of these reasons were lies, as dissatisfying as the answers were to her.

"You should just go get yourself a boyfriend."

Honorico clawed at something fascinating, then rubbed his cheek down into it like he and it must become one. Usually after he did this he came in smelling like a decomposing bird, which I have come to know has a distinct odor. I couldn't wait to see what had perished back there this time.

"If there were boyfriends in cages for me to select from, I would have adopted one of those instead."

"You know what I mean."

"As long as he had his papers," I deflected.

"When's the last time you went on a date?"

I dug my feet into the grass, picking up blades with my toes, destroying the habitat of many a beetle and lightning bug. I didn't look at her. "It's been a while. But I'm not really into that right now."

"Men?"

"Dating. I just don't feel like it."

This never sits well with married people. They want you on the same life course as them, I suppose so they don't get left behind, and so there are allies they can call when all the single people are out there dancing and having sex with attractive people. They want you to buy into the illusion of their fulfillment, suck you into their monotony, and then swallow you as an individual until death do you part. I sensed her discomfort.

"But you said you were lonely." Of course it's also possible she could have just been concerned I was going to drive into my garage, shut the door, and put myself to sleep.

"Yeah, but now I have Honorico," I grinned. He stopped whatever he was doing to look back at me, either because he heard his name or because he felt the same sentiment ride along on the breeze and down his back like a shiver. He smiled back at me, then went about his very serious business involving where he should pee this time.

"Should I be worried?" I felt her look at me as I squinted out to the field.

"No," I answered firmly.

Cherie rubbed her side and made a groan I thought might mean she was in labor. Her stomach protruded enough she leaned on it like she was bellying up to a bar. "Ooh, I think we need to go for banana splits."

"Got a craving?"

"No way. I hate banana splits."

She got me. "Explain to me then why we need to eat them."

"Because I have cramps." She rubbed a little harder and moved her unborn baby out of her ribs like she was shooing a cat.

"Banana splits cure cramps?"

"No one's ever told you to eat a banana when you've gotten a cramp?"

I realized then I was the smarter of us two. "Let me get this straight. You eat a banana split every time your toe cramps up?"

"Not my toe, silly. My stomach."

"I think you're confusing muscle cramps and contractions."

"I know the difference between cramps and contractions, Marin."

"Fine, but a toe cramp and a pain in your side are not the same thing either, and the pains in your side are not prevented by bananas. Further, I am shocked you find banana splits to be a holistic cure." I wasn't sure I was hearing her right, but I knew whatever she was saying and believing was absolutely wrong and potentially dangerous, whatever it was.

"I hate bananas, so the only way I can eat them is with ice cream!" she vociferously defended. And then she began to cry, "And these cramps really, really hurt."

"Sweetheart, are you saying you've had a lot of pains in your side lately?" I tried to calm her.

"Just the last couple of days."

"You've had contractions for two days and all you're doing is eating banana splits?"

"They aren't contractions. They're cramps." But then she turned away, embarrassed. It was like a light bulb popped on in her birth canal and it occurred to her she was probably going to have a baby very soon. "Oh, shit. They are contractions." Her face went white.

"Either you're in labor, or eating so many banana splits doesn't agree with your digestion." I had to laugh. I've used some pretty creative excuses to eat ice cream for two days, ("There's nothing else to eat in the house," "I have a calcium deficiency," "Crunchy foods give me a headache," "I burned my mouth on a curling iron") but deluding oneself out of delivering a baby had me beat. "Why don't we get you to your doctor?"

She nodded nervously, her eyes turning into big round ovaries. I helped her up from the back step and we got the two of her into her car. I drove her to the hospital, where her husband met us an hour later, and where she delivered a healthy baby boy within fifteen minutes, without drugs, and after having only pushed three times. If we had gone for banana splits instead, she would have spit that thing onto the Dairy Queen floor. It was a good thing she didn't, because I was poised to nickname her son Peanut Buster Parfait and yell it from his little league bleachers.

Quite some time later Jane arrived with a man, not an unnamed Brazilian, who spoke plenty of English. He waited in the lounge area casually reading *Redbook* like he went on plenty of dates to the maternity ward. She assured me he was within her age range, which she informed me years before would always be from ages 25-29, to ensure they "knew what they were doing" while their pants were off together, but not so old they were looking to tie her down. She being 30 now, it was a spectator sport to see how many more years she could maintain this rigorous standard.

Together we peered through the observation window at our friend's new little buddy. The nurses back there were nice enough to wheel him up front so we could make eye contact with him, wag our tongues at the important superstar baby instead of a bunch of boring old commoner newborns.

"What do you think? Will it be you or me next?" Jane asked.

I sneered, "I would say neither."

"No way. I'd love one."

I couldn't believe my ears. This from the girl who had been living month-to-month in her apartment for six years. A lease was too much structure, she said. "A baby? You'd love a baby?" Once when we met at the airport for our girls' getaway, she showed up with her purse and a bag of gummy worms. When I asked her where her luggage was, she said she forgot it at home but would just buy stuff as she needed it. No biggie, and would I care for a gummy worm. That was Jane. Jane was not a mom.

"Marin, eventually we all need someone to take care of."

This was very disappointing to hear.

"But you said you never wanted to be needed."

"Yeah, but a baby is different."

"If you had a baby, you'd never be able to jet off to Rio de Janeiro for Christmas."

She psssshhht'd me. "Who says? I saw plenty of babies there."

"Brazilian babies, Jane."

She ignored me. "Don't you think it's fascinating to see someone from the first day of their lives and know everything about them? Every little thing they laugh at, all the things that they're afraid of, what sort of friends they're drawn to. A baby is the one person in the world you can know the most about, and they aren't going to run away from you for it. They don't have any guards against you. They just are who they are. When you're a mom you get a front row seat to that. It's a very exclusive relationship. You don't have that opportunity with any other person ever in your life." She stared through the window and tapped on the glass. "Hi, little baby new person. Welcome to your shiny new life. Be tough, but not too tough. Fall in love with everyone you meet. You can crash at my place when your folks are being a drag." She made faces through the window. She was so enamored I lost track of the baby and started watching her instead.

She put her big red lips on the glass and kissed a semi-permanent hello to him he could see every time he was close enough. I saw the nurse in the back of the room grimace and shake her head, as though this was quite the hospital violation and not something incredibly sweet. Jane paid no intention, she never did, which is why she's so lovable. She waved just the tips of her fingers and then skipped down the hall to her new mystery man whose name I would make no point to memorize until his third appearance in our lives. I'd learned they're all pretty temporary.

I turned and put my forehead on the glass and watched him watch me. I know at that age, not quite a day, they can't see very far, and so odds are if he saw me at all I was just a big blob of shadows to him. I smiled anyway, sighed my concerns for him. Yes, be tough but not too tough. I couldn't think of any better advice for the kid. Somewhere around puberty we become too tough. I know I had. I hoped he would leave a little room for pain to squeeze in, or else like the rest of us he would protect himself and thereby detour from people and experiences that could really make his life great. We do this. We are so safe we are barely alive.

The baby was just a baby. I know that. I knew that then. I was fully conscious of the facts at the time. I knew if he even had thoughts they were more like emotions and not words. They were the most basic of human urges and reactions, not articulated in his mind in any other way except "to cry or not to cry." I know that. I'm not crazy. But I'm telling you, that kid spoke to me.

We locked eyes. Sure, his were beady and surrounded by baby chub that screamed "my mother only feeds me banana splits," but he was definitely looking at me. I whispered, "What a weird fuckin' day, huh, kid?" And then, like a bug bit me, I got a message from Pat. I don't know what he was saying exactly, whether he loved me or just wanted to say "what's up?" or that I looked pretty that day, or maybe I should watch my language around a newborn baby. I just knew he was there, in the baby's eyes. I know it still, it was him. I started to cry because I could feel him all around me then, like he was now a love cloud floating in my personal aura where there was plain old oxygen a second earlier. I realized if he was a love cloud that meant he was not a tangible being anymore, and it hit me that this would mean he was probably dead.

I know how this sounds, like I'm legally insane. It feels as weird to me as it does for you to read it that in one paragraph's time I can explain that my lover in apparition form used a baby as a medium to visit me from beyond. I won't say that he said "boo" in my ear, because he did not. I did not get a chill and the lights didn't flicker. He didn't slide a penny up a door or anything. This was not that kind of moment. I am just certain the sensation all over my body and the intensity in this baby's face was a signal for me to let go of Pat, in a way that one knows but cannot verify except to say we all have had intimate experiences with something higher that don't need explaining. In fact no amount of detail and convincing delivery can explain them. You know them when you feel them.

I thought this moment through for weeks after, trying to make sense of it or recreate it in the nervous quiet of the early morning hours. I would lay in bed at three or so, thinking that sort of stillness was the perfect time for Pat to contact me. I meditated on his image and the list of memories I'd made not too long before, then shut my eyes and told him secrets that only felt safe then to tell.

I shoplifted food in college. Frequently.

My parents' divorce still makes me cry, twenty years later.

Sometimes when I'm driving on the freeway I have a weird fantasy of jerking the wheel as hard as I can to the left so that the car flips, and I probably die.

I have had more unprotected sex than protected sex in my lifetime.

My entire résumé is filled with lies.

When I was 23 I waited outside my boyfriend's house in a hooded sweatshirt in order to catch him cheating. I did this for six straight nights. When I finally caught him and had what I needed to justify dumping him, I still took him back without even hearing him apologize.

I am a good singer but will never have the courage to show anyone.

Even though I say women are too hard on themselves, I have on ten or fifteen occasions thrown up my food on purpose.

I am just as afraid of someone knowing these things about me as I am of never having anyone I can believe in enough to tell.

And that's what it's all really about, isn't it? We seek so hard for someone to know us, and then we barrier ourselves as though no one is deserving.

I concentrated on Pat's image every night for two weeks and that psychic-baby feeling never returned. That adrenaline rush followed by a warm calm, I have never felt it since that day at the maternity ward. Sometimes when I visit the baby and hold him up close, I sense there is a bond there, a knowing depth in his eyes. Maybe he remembers being a conduit that day, but Pat is no longer with him. But then I realize he's just gassy, and he is just a plain old baby now.

Eventually it was time. Skud's hadn't seen my butt in its seats since the night I met Pat. I had thought about going a million times in the months prior. First I wanted to go because I was lonesome, maybe it would feel like Pat was there. Then I wanted to go because it reminded me of simpler times, when death wasn't something that came up in my internal dialog every minute of every day. Another day I was sure I was over the hump, that my worst days were behind me, and I should go and sit at the bar so that Pat, wherever he was, would be proud of me. But then I got a block away and feared I would walk in, Pat would be sitting there in his Army cap talking up another lonely girl, and I would melt down into a puddle of pity. I didn't know he was dead, after all. I did, but a day-old baby's eyes aren't exactly the same thing as the military showing up at your door with a folded, triangular flag.

Then one day the sun was shining like it sprang directly from my front yard. Honorico and I put on shorts and washed the car in the driveway with early nineties grunge rock blaring from a boom box that, come to think of it, might also have been from the early nineties. I was alive again, and so I thought that might be the perfect time to pop in and see my old friends, the nameless bartenders.

Time to move forward.

This isn't to say I wasn't nervous. I will admit I slammed a beer before even getting there just to slip into my "ah, fuck it" persona. The whole drive over I rubbed and twisted my neck in odd angles to work out the anxiety kinks that seem to appear instantaneously during moments like these. I forgot to turn on that part of the brain that requires no conscious thought in order to walk, and so my feet moved like clown shoes through the gravel parking lot. I tripped once, then did that thing where you look back to see whatever it was you tripped over, like that was going to take away the comedy of the moment, and lucky observers would excuse you for looking like an idiot, like it was the curb's fault I didn't see it. This of course only made my heart beat harder.

Here we were during baseball season and my watering hole was packed. I found a seat nowhere near where Pat and I met, because that would be too weird, and because I'm not an Italian widow. I don't need to mourn so melodramatically. I sat on the other end completely and watched as his bar stool remained empty the entire duration of the game, and I was fine with it.

Beers and beers in, the Brewers dominated innings and innings, and the bar gained momentum. Patrons nearby high-fived me after every home run, and one insisted we take a shot for every strikeout. This was a stellar pitching day for our team, and so there was much whiskey poured. I was feeling good. We were all feeling good. It was the point in the cycle of Midwestern living when we have forgotten the tension of winter, when we strain our muscles to keep warm and our hearts beat in double time to keep blood flowing to the vulnerable outer limits of our fingers, toes, and noses. The tension gives way to relaxed sighs and those sorts of warm yawns that are accompanied by a sweet and lazy groan that oozes out from a new, slower beating heart that grew in right around the time the ivy and dandelions sprang up. Everyone you encounter deserves a smile and howdy-do, and naturally strangers in bars are much more generous with celebratory booze. We enjoyed a steady hum of peaceful solidarity, punctuated by the occasional double play or stolen base and the subsequent ruckus.

All was well.

Then a man stumbled from the bathroom and lost his way. Originally he was sitting over closer to me but got turned around on his way back. We all tend to lose our internal compass after that many beers. I watched as he tried to sit right where Pat sat that fateful evening, when my life changed, when everything changed. The man's eyelids hung so low it was clear once his legs could maneuver the very difficult task of sitting down on the stool, he would put his head down and it would be lights-out for him. I wondered which of his friends down my way would be responsible for that mess once the game was over.

But it never came to that, thank goodness. The bartender, who had greeted me as "Mare" on my way in, stopped the drunkard before he could slide a second butt cheek on. "Hey, buddy, you're going to have to find somewhere else to sit." Terse but polite, no one I would mess with.

"There's nobody sitting here," the fellow slurred.

"There are plenty of other seats down there," thumbing his way back toward me, "you're just going to have to pick another one." The bartender wiped things down that didn't need wiping, a time tested tactic so as not to appear confrontational, but an unmistakable signal he meant business. The drunk didn't argue, just blew a burp out the side of his mouth and made his way back to his original seat. The bartender didn't make a fuss, just said, "Thank you, sir," and collected dollars here and there along the bartop.

A few minutes later he refilled my Guinness. He leaned on an elbow as we waited for the first pull to settle. "How's it going, Marin?"

"I'm well, how are you?" I meant it. All of it.

He scanned the bar for anyone in need, "Yeah, you know. I'm good. We're moving into the slow season soon." Drinkers tended to stay outdoors during the warmer months, cawing their revelry into the Lake Michigan surf.

"Can I ask you a question?"

"Anything, my dear."

"Why is that seat off limits?"

"Pat's seat?" My heart stopped. I literally felt it stop. That was the first time I'd heard his name outside the walls of my thoughts in months. In two whole seasons.

I swallowed, nodded.

Bartender's face darkened. "If Pat can't sit in that seat, no one can," and then he looked away to compose himself.

His pain aside, this was exactly what I needed to hear. He turned back to look me in the eye in a matter of fact way, as though thems were the breaks and anyone who didn't understand would get an earful from him, and somewhere in there the words "sacrifice" and "selfless duty" would come up. It was a rush in the worst way, but I needed him to say those words when he did.

I gave him an approving smile and said nothing else.

The game ended a while a later, a win for the Brewers, and so the city walked a little lighter in their flip-flops. I did, too. The drunks moved on to the places they go to celebrate harder, other bars, and I supposed it was my turn to move on as well. I felt no pain, no regret, no loss. I felt renewed.

Before I got up from my seat I took this momentary high and ran with it. I signaled the bartender over with a little wave. I put some cash down for him and he skipped over to say thank you. I hesitated at first, then went for it. "I'm sorry. I have to ask you a question, and I'm sorry if this is embarrassing. I assure you it's as awkward for you me as it is for you."

He smiled and crossed his arms. "Okay, I'm ready. Go for it."

"I've been coming here for years and, well, what the hell is your name?"

He laughed and leaned back, miming a gunshot to the heart. "Ugh, that's rough."

"I know. I've felt bad all this time. And the more time passed, the more uncomfortable it would get to ask you. I kept waiting to overhear someone else say it, but no one ever did. The next thing I know it's years later and you are calling me 'Mare' for short, and I'm calling you 'Buddy.'"

He granted me a reprieve. "It's Hank."

I reached out my hand to his and he was forgiving enough to shake it. "It's nice to finally meet you, Hank."

"And you as well."

It was a beautiful day.

And then it was time to go. Honorico needed his dinner.

Daylight streamed through the windows in stiff beams, and I felt their call. I grabbed my things and headed toward the blinding glow, trusting whatever was on the other side. On the way out, without thinking about it or turning on the part of my brain that controls what my arms do, I ran my hand along the smooth, worn seat of Pat's barstool.

Just a quick hello before I blended back into the world.

CPSIA information can be obtained at www.ICGtesting.com

226421LV00001B/4/P